T0103532

WHEN I FOUND INFINITY

WHEN I FOUND INFINITY

AR PANDEY

PARTRIDGE

Copyright © 2016 by Ar Pandey.

| ISBN: | Softcover | 978-1-4828-8580-4 |
| | eBook | 978-1-4828-8579-8 |

All rights reserved. No part of this book may be used or reproduced by any means, graphic, electronic, or mechanical, including photocopying, recording, taping or by any information storage retrieval system without the written permission of the author except in the case of brief quotations embodied in critical articles and reviews.

Because of the dynamic nature of the Internet, any web addresses or links contained in this book may have changed since publication and may no longer be valid. The views expressed in this work are solely those of the author and do not necessarily reflect the views of the publisher, and the publisher hereby disclaims any responsibility for them.

Print information available on the last page.

To order additional copies of this book, contact
Partridge India
000 800 10062 62
orders.india@partridgepublishing.com

www.partridgepublishing.com/india

We all meet different kinds of people during our school days. Some come in our lives and go. Some come and stay. This one is for all of them.

ACKNOWLEDGEMENTS

This book would have stayed in my cupboard if I would not have been helped and guided by few people.

This book would have been incomplete without the help and support of partridge publishers who made this book a reality. I am eternally thankful to them.

My parents, for their constant support. Everyone knows that how sacrificing and selfless love they shower upon us.

My elder brother, ankit for his support.

The only person who knew about this project completely was akshita. She had her bucket full of suggestions which I found very helpful throughout the writing process. Big thanks to her.

Ritwik for his faith on me, aashray for the encouragements, mansi, amol, Sidharth, akash, saurabh, aditya, and whoever who got involved in this project, I owe it to each and every one of you.

And my last thanks to my readers who have bought this book with a faith of finding something which they can enjoy reading. I have tried my best. I wish you a happy reading ahead.

Arpit Pandey
arpitp053@gmail.com

ABOUT THE AUTHOR

Arpit pandey is an eighteen year old teen who hails from bihar. As he has stayed for more than twelve years in dehradun, the capital of uttarakhand, he wrote his first book, "when I found infinity" with dehradun as the backdrop.

A medical aspirant, but that didn't stop him from completing this book which is in your hand.

You can contact him on his email id arpitp053@gmail.com for suggestions and criticisms which will be highly appreciated.

PROLOGUE

"*Such a beautiful night.*" She gazed at the sky. Even I hadn't seen such a clear sky in all my life. And the stars were innumerable. Every constellation had made sure to give its attendance in today's night class. The Doon valley complimented the skies with its lightings.

"It is magical. The way I wanted it to be." She looked at me and gently smiled. The winters had completely set in. it was late at night and we were wearing overcoats. There were some rickshaw pullers playing cards. We stopped to look at them; abusing each other everytime they lost a chance. We whispered to each other about this and giggled softly so that they wouldn't hear us.

Mall road lied calm in front and behind. There was silence, which broke with a dog's howl or a vehicle going down the valley.

Moments just passed. Moments into seconds and seconds into minutes and minutes into memories.

"Say something. All topics covered or what?" I tried to break the silence. She chuckled a bit and quietly came closer and put her hand across my arm.

"Hush! This silence is better than anything."

The road was brightly lit by street lamps and house lights.

"I have been here many times. I have walked these roads. I have seen this place full of snow. But I never felt so pleased before." She spoke softly while we walked. Both of us were feeling cold. We took very short steps. Our teeth clattered a little while our mouth and nose passed out the vapours when we breathed.

I noticed her smile and the reddened nose. 'Santa Claus of my life!' I smiled.

"what are you smiling at?" "It's nothing." "what! tell me!" "I told you. It's nothing, just your...nose." she pushed me gently away. "huh!"

They both disappeared the same way they had appeared; suddenly.

My eyes saw the rotating ceiling fan. There was no one except a pillow beside me and it was no winter season. We don't live ideal lives, do we?

* * * * *

ONE

Many a times, when I sat on the bench provided by the municipal corporation near my house at vasant vihar in the dehradun valley, I came across people of various moods and statures. Last time when I had taken my usual seat on the bench, a drunkard had managed to cross the road haphazardly, to finally lie under my bench. Sometimes there were elderly people, strolling about the footpath, discussing the very same topic –"things were not like this when we were young." A smile would spread across my face. *Things are really not the same.* It was the month of june and my higher secondary was passed and completed. The memories were still present and they would always come and linger untill I used to rise up and go straight towards my home. Needless to say, I had become gloomy. "six months have gone by and nothing is present except the sad face and the feeling to go back and relish them once again." But that was another of my fantasies. Some high school romances are meant to end.

we had always followed this custom about having this family dinner on fridays. It kept us tied. Father's profession used to hamper this ritual but later he had also started to manage them.

"So, how are the Sharma's doing?", he asked cheerfully. "Same story, different day." I barked out. The breakup had altered my mood completely. I was no more a person of tolerance but a machine of mood swings. "Talking loudly, shouting on us will not change the fact that your friend will never talk with you." This 'friend' was none other than her. One thing you need to understand about indian families. You just cannot divulge informations about your relationships, and that too on a dinner. So, I had just told them that there was one best friend of mine who was not talking to me and had ended oour friendship.

"But after so many days, why do you keep remembering that friend of yours who, for sure, must not be remembering you this bad as you are?" He was bang on point, my father, perhaps that person might not be remembering me this much. I was living in an illusion that I am being missed. I was badly mistaken and it was all my fault. No one was guilty except this boy of eighteen.

I made my way up to my bedroom and lied down. I stared at the contacts list in the dark room. It still showed her name. Clearly written with a smiling emoticon afterwards – 'aishani'. I had tried to delete the contact and was quite successful a couple of times and had even tried to make my mind say – aishani is bad, hate her, aishani is bad, hate her. The mind and heart, both replied the same- not happening buddy. I opened my instant messenger and saw her profile. The display picture was gone and so were those status which once bloomed with the emoticons of hearts and kisses. I never had the guts to block her from my contacts but she had somehow acquired them. She had blocked me from that very day, last day of january.

"arav, I think we should give free space to each other. I know that this might sound a bit harsh but let's see, let's see if our love can prove itself." She said teasingly, but she was seriously speaking about taking a break. "And to make this more concrete, we shall not be in touch for two months. I am giving my phone to mummy." Was she going mad? Was she in her senses?

I was taken aback. Two months! How will I be able to stay without her for straight two months! I could have easily said yes if she had been anyone else, even Supriya, who was my best friend, but not her, not aishani, aishani was more than a friend, more than love, but above all, my constant for over five months.

"this is the time when I will be needing you the most aishani. I don't know what life will show me in the coming days, but I need your support. A support, which only you can give. But the same person is saying me that I would be gone? Are you not thinking anything about us? Every promise has been undone? Is this a way of testing my love for you? If that's the thing, then it's not good. Not at all good."

The clock ticked quietly at the back while the emotions oozed out through words.

"I know that my love loves me this much but you also have to study no? your board exams are just in a month and you need to study and i dont want you to keep thinking about me and degrade your performance. You have to be the best and have to become topper! Imagine aishani! Your boyfriend is a topper, how wonderful would that feel!"

3

"I will never ever think of you as a distraction for me. How can I even think of that! You were the one who lifted from a phase of sadness and made me enjoy the pleasures of life. You were the one who told me to showcase my talents in the competition. You are my biggest blessing, my infinity."

But but but, who can even think of defeating a girl in a conversation. "enough of your romantic talks Mr arav Sharma. I am not listening to all of this and I am going offline and will not come till the month of march and that is final. Now bye bye and study. Your preboards were not even good, they were infact bad, not even bad but worse, worse for a person like you. Its time that you study hard." And she hung up, not giving me an oppurtunity to even speak further. She was right though. I had failed in chemistry and that too in the preboards. That was the most humiliating thing in all of my life as a student. The teachers and the students as well as the juniors were in big shock. "arav Sharma has failed in chemistry! Can you believe that?" "He was a topper kind of a guy no?" "I have heard that he has started smoking and has not been studying at all!" Etc and more etc, It takes many years to build a reputation but it takes just a wink of an eye to destroy it and bring it down to nothing. I was no exception, I was never an exception about anything. Just a person who tried to put his hand in everything and anything and failing in it.

This revelation about failing was the toughest job. Throughout my way from the school, I was searching for the proper words and a proper tone to bring this news down. I kept practising the scene but mother was unpredictable when it came on results. Sometimes she would just leave it when a hundred was achieved and sometimes would celebrate about it while sometimes even a mark would hurt her so much that she would curse me and say that I will become a watchman in the future. Mind you, she said these when I had got the third position. Needless to say, she was a typical Indian mother. So when I reached and parked my *activa,* she bombarded me with questions, "how are the marks this time? how much in physics? You always get less marks, I am worried that you might loose the ninety percent mark in the boards." "mummy, I have failed in chemistry, I have got twenty five out of seventy." There was this silence. A very deafening mute. She was staring at me as if I had just told the end about the universe she moved away and sat on the dining chair. I went upstairs to change. I knew that I will be confronted any moment now onwards. Frankly speaking, I was waiting for it. I was just thinking, what will the words sound?

"That was the last thing which I had expected from you, atleast you could have passed, I dont know whats going to happen in the boards, i am scared for your future, boy, really scared now." she was calm till this point, when she suddenly shouted- "Find yourself a chemistry teacher as soon as you can, ask from your silly friends, where they go, ask and tell me latest by evening." And she slammed the door shut and I was there standing, ashamed and embarrased. All the friends with whom I used to call, most of their tuitions had ended and it was very difficult to find a tutor who would teach me chemistry in about twenty days. Before I had conversed with aishani, I messaged my best friend, my last hope, Supriya-

Arav: "supriyaaaa! help!!"

supriya_097:yes boss!

Arav: please! no jokes right now, find me a tutor!please!

supriya_097:what happened but?

Arav: I will call you later and tell everything but firstly, you find me a tutor as soon as possible. Where do you go by the way?

supriya_097:okay okay, relax bro. I go to Maam sharmila, your chemistry teacher.

Arav: Can I come? please give the contact number, please please please, you are my best sister.

supriya_097:dont butter me bro, I have messaged her number, good luck. I will talk to you later. bye bye.

As if my luck was laughing at me and saying loudly to me that your good days were gone and now all that was left would be hardships.

But you can't expect spring all round the year. Autumn does come and comes quickly.

* * * * *

TWO

Maam Sharmila ahluwalia was a very good teacher indeed, I personally liked her teaching style and the fact that she knew her subject so well used to impress me everytime. The amount of knowledge acquired by her in such a young age was impeccable. Organic, physical or inorganic, she had every answers on her finger tips. Yet, during the school hours, she used to put up a very stern and a very uninterested face while teaching. It was not her fault. The children had become notorious as ever and their innocent tricks were not innocent anymore.

Maam Ahluwalia lived in a posch colony in the outskirts of the city, in a comparavitively sophisticated society of rich business class. I saw many vehicles parked outside the gate. That was the one, I said to myself. "lets go inside brother, lets see whats going to happen."

There was a spacious lawn neatly mowed with different flowers, the house itself was quite huge, with marble flooring even in the garage where usually, its kept raw. Clearly, maam was rich. Behind the audi car, Maam was teaching kids in her garage. Two big wooden desks had been put up and round chairs were placed around it and a white board hung on the wall completed this classroom. The clock struck five and the children moved out. Supriya was there too. She was a class younger than me. We met during an inter school singing competition when she was given the position next to me and from there on, our bond had grown in leaps and bounds. A warm feeling which comes from a sister had come at the very instance when we first talked. Triangular face with brown eyes with a natural blush on her cheeks, she was always excited to do everything she could during school hours. "so you made it bro, welcome!" she teased. "haha, very funny no? anyways thank you for helping your big silly brother everytime, may you be blessed with a boyfriend soon!" we laughed. She was the only person in my entire friend circle who knew about aishani. I felt that she was the only one I could trust and who would never say a word to anyone. When I had first told her about aishani, she said-"bro, you are drunk, get some sleep and let me sleep as well", in a very made up sleepy voice. "stupid, its true. Its as true as calling you the biggest retard in the world." "shut up bro! And how in the world you came across aishani! I mean seriously, aishani!? she is north and you are south, she is careless and dumb and stupid and everything. How can you just possibly.." And she started laughing. Oh god, how difficult it is to convince that you are actually in love or anything related to it. The more you try, the harder it gets and harder the laughs. "May I interrupt your laughter?" I was getting annoyed. "oh! sorry bro, really sorry. Please tell when all of this happened and please tell this in detail so that I can tell this to all my friends who think that "arav bhaiya" is not into all this stuff." I knew that she was joking but, when you get the stimulus of love for the first time, you turn cautious about every move which you make. "I will assassin you if you even dream of telling this thing to even yourself. Promise me that you wont be sharing this to anyone, I repeat no one, not even your dog coco." "I was joking bro, I will not tell this to anyone, you know that." "hmm hmm I know. I will tell everything about aishani, lets meet tomorrow at *buddha temple* at nine sharp."

Buddha temple was a hotspot among all the "love birds" of the doon valley. I had never gone with aishani there. The lush greens and huge forests behind the temple kept the place cool throughout. I remember those times when I used to come with my parents on our two wheeler and would sit beneath one of the trees and sleep during the afternoons. We used to eat donuts from the shop which was inside the temple's campus. It was lovely, not because of its taste but because that time, I used to come there just because of those donuts which I never used to find anywhere else in the entire city. Father never used to eat those, he would tease us by making faces and telling all those ill effects of eating them. "Daddy! why you always say this." A nine year old arav Sharma used to angrily speak to his father. But that anger was good, that anger used to make mummy and daddy smile and laugh even more, that anger used to vanish as soon as I used to gulp down a piece of yummy donuts. I missed that anger. I had reached the temple on time, as planned. But madam supriya was nowhere. Always late, she was.

Meanwhile I decide to stroll around the campus. It felt as if nothing had changed. The stupa still looked the same and the statue of lord buddha coming down from the heaven on the top of the monastery still shined. The shops had changed though. The donut shopped had changed into a cafe and many new clothes shop had also come up. But the peace, that peace was still present. Supriya came after I had checked every shop and had tried to bargain for a tracksuit, but I eventually failed, the shopkeeper was a tough competition for me.

black jacket and blue denims with black boots, Supriya knew how to dress properly, meanwhile I was in a grey trouser and a full sleeve shirt with a blue half jacket with some local brand's shoes providing me, lets just say, satisfactory amount of comfort. "you are never good in dressing up bro, never ever." "As if I am hearing this for the first time." she chuckled. "lets take something to eat first, there is a long story you will be hearing today."

Excited as ever, we went to the "nepali's" which was an excellent place for dimsums and spring rolls and all kinds of soups. Dimsums, lets just say is one of the most loved food by the people of doon. They love dimsums, whether they are steamed or whether they are fried on charcoal or fried, every kind of dimsum had its own loyal followers. I had tasted every kind of dimsum but the steamed one was the best. "one can judhge the quality of a dimsum if you can see the vegetables inside it." said the golden rule which our sports teacher had once said. The dimsums in hand passed this test and so we sat on the grass. Winters had aravrived and the heat from the sun only made it pleasant and the mood drowsy. "So, start from the beginning bro, where it all started?"

"It was the month of july and our school was getting ready for *the panache,* which was an inter school festival held at one of the most famous schools of dehradun, St Harrison's College. You know *na* that our school is ever enthusiastic about participating in every festival and this was no exception. The musical group was formed, the quiz team was choosen, the dancers were chereographed, the photography duo was chosen and the actors were trained for over a month. The campus used to bloom after the school had ended. Noises, shouts, giggles, everything used to echo during that time inside our auditorium. Music room had become a studio with synthesizers and amplifiers and electric guitars. The team had to perform a meadley on the *famous bollywood and Hollywood singers.* After minor hiccups, they eventually had got the rhythmn right. The dance group was doing flawless and the photographers were ready to create a masterpiece from their sceneries."

"and the quiz team?" supriya said after gulping down an entire dimsum. "There I was, in the quiz team, one thing you got to realize about quizzing, is that, its always unpredictable." I laughed at this. Quizzes had been always that ways. Sometimes, they ask about the radius of jupiter and sometimes they ask about the new flick releasing this *diwali,* so there were pretty slim chances of knowing what will be asked in the quiz. The preliminary rounds which was conducted at almost every quiz was the most annoying of it all. All the tough questions of the world were asked in this round and the remaining quiz looked like a fifth standard general knowledge book. "sir, why they do this everytime? why do they ask the impossible in the prelims." Our teacher used to laugh and say –"*hota hai hota hai.*"

Meanwhile, we had been given yearbooks which which we had to learn, some more magazines, some more journals, some more newspapers and finally some more sleepless nights. Raghvendra, which was my partner was a serious nerd. Though he knew that he would not be able to learn all of this in all of his life, he had given the most confident of smiles that I had ever seen. I had asked him once – "Learned the book?" He said in a most innocent tone-"How can I?" "Basterd", I muttered.

The day had finally come when we had to go the festival. *The panache* was a one day academic cum cultural festival held at the st Harrison's college. From the past many years, they had been holding this event and this was the first time when when our school had been invited. The excitement was too much. We reached the college at seven. Every one's mouth stood wide open when we saw the auditorium. *The past welcomes you to the future,* it said. Kurt cobain, Al pacino, Elvis Presley, Charlie Chaplin came back to life on the flexes made by the students of the college. And at the centre of the stage, there was its symbol, a shining P with flames all around the syllable. The whole ambience promised a wonderful day ahead. "excuse me arav, can you please help me carry my clothes to the green room?",a short heighted girl stood before me, her eyes were down, looking at the floor and her face had this different but strong presence of innocence. And her eyes, when I saw were brown, beautiful brown eyes. I had known her by name for many days but had never met personally. She was a wonderful dancer, that I had heard from the other dancers and that she would be the lead dancer of their performance at the panache. Her name was aishani.

"Sure aishani, no problem, you are our lead dancer, anything for you." she just smiled and we walked outside the auditorium. The weather had been pleasant since morning, clouds had come and go. It started raining as we stepped out of the auditorium. I picked oe of the umbrellas, "come on aishani, lets go" I dont know why she hesitated. "No, its okay, I will wait for the rain to stop." "Oh come on aishani, lets go fast, you have to change as soon as you can!" she came inside the big blue umbrella with a wooden handle tightly clutched by me. We had to make our way all the way around the auditorium to reach the green room allotted to our school. Neither of us spoke and we quickly reached the room. I just smiled after dropping her apparels and I closed the door and went back to the audi.

* * * * *

THREE

"Hey! thats not fair!", supriya said during the recess, while I enjoyed a nice bite of crispy patties of her money. "gotcha!", and Ronit managed to snatch half of it from my hand. "what the hell man!" "hey! you dont have that right to say." he laughed and feasted on that free patties. everyday, supriya and I used to stand next to the canteen window and would try to crash the buyer. Most of the times, it would lead to the loss of food but we enjoyed during that. "oh! look look! arushi is purchasing *bun-tikki* for us." we hooted. "Not this time guys.." and she managed to run past us. The memories of aishani had faded away and these daily laughs and gags had taken over. Aishani was a reserved kind of a girl. Except for the dance at the panache, she was hardly seen outside her classroom. She had few friends but all of them were intovert like her. More over it never felt right to talk to her just because we had shared an umbrella together. That sounded odd to me.

Inter house dance competition was announced to take place at the end of august. All the houses had gathered their teams. Our house, *feathers* decided to put up a religious dance, dedicated to lord *shankar*. During one of the morning assembly, my house mistress approached me, "Son, we are depicting lord shiva in our dance sitting with the goddess Parvati, so I was wondering if you could take this role." I was puzzled. No one had ever approached me to enact something for a performance. I was particularly scared of the stage. "Thank you maam but I dont think that I am the right person for the job." She insisted. I dont know why she was insisting so much. Did I looked thin or anything? I stared down. I agreed though, it didnt feel good to reject a teacher's request. "we will begin from today, after the school gets over. We are lagging behind others. Do you know that girl? aishani, I think of *petals* house, she is training her house and they are good, really good."

she said more about the other houses but I hardly noticed one or two things after the name-aishani. There was something so serene and tranquil about this name which tickled my sensations. aishani, for me sounded religious, something which, if was to be understood, one had to go down into it and keep going untill he had found about her. The name made me feel to dive into her and stay there.

I felt pretty awkward just sitting in the middle and see the dancers dancing around me. The practices were going on and days had passed. I was still sitting and watching them. "someone please kill me."

our dancers were going along well. They tried to perfect various *mudras* we all knew that it takes ages to perfect and not a month.

My birthday came on a saturday this time. So, I was not wished by the entire school like most time, but I decided to give chocolates to each of those who were staying back for the dance. It was the last day of the practice and on monday was the big day. Hurriedly, I went to the canteen, "ram bhaiya, give me fifty of your rare good chocolates." He beamed at me-"every chocolate sold by me is a good one *bhaisab*." "haha, what a joke!" I giggled at my own thought.

Ignoring his sly remarks, I collected the chocolates and distributed among my housemates. Then I went to *leaves* and then to *wings* and now I made my way to *petals*. If someone would have asked me, why are you giving these children chocolates worth rupees ten each who dont even know you, I would have proudly said that to see aishani once more talking to me was all the reason I could have given. The house was practising in the activity room at the back of the junior building. I knocked and saw them finally concluding their last step. "well done guys, nailed it, now we just have to replicate this on the stage on monday. You were excellent aishani, keep it up." aishani just gave a polite nod and her eyes were down, looking at the floor. "ohh dear, come in." maam abha glanced at the intruder of their practice. "maam, today is my birthday." that was spoken bluntily. "happy birthday arav, come on, give me the chocolate, I demand two."

> *Transfixed at her eyes, perplexed by their charm those eyes are love, they mean to lovingly harm.....*

She came and shrugged my shoulders. "come on! what are you thinking? chocolate please!" A quite and shy aishani had changed into a bubbly one, she was asking for chocolates as if she had known that toaday was my birthday and that I would get her a chocolate. Coming quickly back from my deep train of thoughts, I gave her two bars and moved ahead to give it to others.

Gut feeling said she wanted to talk with me, mind said, do what you had to do and get out, heart was mum, confused and perplexed. It looks voluntary from the outside but it's involuntary from the inside. Never in our control. Never ever.

Returning home, I called Supriya and loudly said- "Supriya, give me aishani number quickly, right now, right now." I had wanted this thing to complete in one shot. It felt so uneasy about asking for her number. That feeling is aptly termed Goosebumps.

"You okay bro?"

"I am fine. Just give me the number."

I now had the number on my display screen. Ten randomly arranged digits which would connect me with aishani. Here we go; here we go, come on, just a thank-you-for-your-wishes kind of a call.

The ringer came into life. It rang once, then again, and again. With each ring, my heartbeat paced up. It kept ringing till a silence appeared on the line and then it followed a "hello?"

"Hello aishani, it's me, arav." Why I was shivering! "Arav, don't, don't, relax buddy, talk nicely, nice and easy boy, nice and easy.

"Hiiii arav, how are you?

"I am good…. I just wanted to thank you for your good wishes. That was wonderful…"

"You are always welcome arav and no need to say thanks. Friends never thank each other."

"Friends?" who said that we were friends, I thought, we had hardly talked four sentences and we were friends!

It reminded me of an old movie whose protagonist had said to his friend who would eventually be his lady love- *dosti ka ek usool hota hai madam, no sorry, no thank you.*

"Are you still there on the phone?" My filmy thoughts had lasted for more than thirty seconds. "Yes, yes I am." Another period of silence. What to speak? What to speak? Should I ask whether she liked old music or new music? Or should I ask if she liked *mohabattein* more than *dilwale dulhaniya le jayenge*? I asked something serious instead. Courtesy- my heart.

"Why do you stay so reserved? I mean, why do you prefer seclusion?"

I knew that a little period of silence would follow and it did followed. I could faintly make out that she was breathing and thinking about it.

"I don't know, maybe because I like to keep myself a mystery. A mystery so that no one is able to make out who the real me is and hence will not be able to judge any of my thoughts and will not be able to tell, which path I might choose."

I felt attracted by this. It was something, which I had never heard from a person. It was different. Aishani was different. "Am I the only one telling out secrets *haa?* You are no less than a surprise package arav, I can sense that. You must be having some story. Everyone has a story. And I am interested to hear."

I told her that I would her about my "story" at night. I decided to go for a walk. "Walking and you? Sun has changed its direction or is it just me?" Mummy could always be counted upon for sarcasm.

The outside was calm. Our colony hardly interacted with each other. The road looked perpetually deserted. I wondered when these parked cars moved which were parked inside the houses.

I clicked pictures of the flowers and the distorted clouds. Today, they looked beautiful. Today, I saw a silver lining. Today, everything was picture perfect. I kept thinking about the promise I had done. *I would be telling her my story.* But what was my story? What could possibly my story? What would I tell her? I kept thinking while sitting on the bench provided by MDDA. Nothing much had happened in my seventeen years of existence.

An ordinary school life. Going, studying and coming back. Only this year had I participated in the quizzes. I felt jealous towards those who had so many friends. I felt lonely during the recess when I had no one to talk. I would just stand near the stage, eat my lunch and then go back to the class. This was my routine. It was not that I hadn't tried to make friends with the students. It was just that, they became bored with my company and they eventually left my side. Sometimes, they would hello and move ahead. I was nothing more than a hello for many.

Baffling with thoughts, I returned home. I ate my dinner hastily. At nine, I had to call her as we had planned.

"are you ready with your story?" She excitedly said.

"what you want to hear? I don't have much to say. I was born today some seventeen years ago and after that, nothing much has happened except my height."

"arav, what is a story? Tell me."

"stories are a collection of incidents which take place with people." "Exactly. Tell me incidents about your life. And you are speaking, no excuses given or taken."

"Okay, let me think. I was born in the city of banaras."

"wow arav, you are from banaras! *Banarasi babu haa!'*" She chuckled.

"I had enough of that banarasi babu aishani." I grinned. "okay sorry *banarasi babu.*" And there she went teasing again. I told her to shut up. I said that I didn't like it. I was liking it more and more.

I told her about my family, how we had come from banaras to doon for a better living. The initial struggles which an immigrant faces, trying to adjust to the new surrounding, trying to adjust to a new lifestyle. Then my difficulties in finding a school for myself, when I failed most of the entrance tests and finally got admitted to *Vincent academy* in class three. I tried to tell her in the most interesting way, so that she doesn't get bored like everyone else with whom I had tried, they had stopped this story within four sentences. Not this time, it didn't happened this time. I completed my entire life story in fifteen minutes. She would keep replying "hmm" and *ohh's and really's,* showing her interest. "that was one of the most interesting life story I have ever heard. Why were you saying that your life will sound boring? It was so intriguing." It felt nice to hear that. Someone liked my story.

"now its your turn to tell." I giggled. Lets see what she would say. Time was flowing smoothly, the night was increasing the warmth as the conversation progressed.

"I come from Gujarat, where my dad had a cotton mill. Due to loss in the trade, we came to doon to start a new business as my maternal uncle is a well known merchant here, so he helped up and now we are living here for the past eight years. Since I am the elder sister, so I was the one who would act brave and take care of my little sister *Aahana*. She would demand and she would get anything but I was told how to be content with whatever I had. I wanted many things which *aahana* had got but……" And there was a moment of quietness. She must have started thinking about those moments, those little sacrifices which every elder sibling had to do. And though most of it looked childish from a mature perspective, it was serious for a child. "Its not mandatory for an elder one to sacrifice every time. Is it?"

I had no experience of these type of questions and what should be the correct response to these "is it?" type of questions. If I said no, then maybe she would feel that I was offending her sister and a yes would have meant an end to this talk. I tried-"maybe aishani, maybe you were being tested and perhaps there is something in store for you in the future!" That answer, I felt had brought a smile on her face. A crooked smile spread across my face, "thank you for that arav. I needed it."

"will meet you on Monday at the dance competition. All the best to you aishani." "thanks and same to you." She said, lowering her voice.

The following Sunday was spent in helping mummy in the dusting work and trying my hand at cooking. I was waiting for the next day, the dance competition, where aishani would make her house win. I resisted myself from calling her. I didn't want myself to look as a desperate person. The slower you go, the better the yield.

I hurriedly reached the school at seven. Our school started at eight but the dancers were called much before as the makeup was to be done and all the stage setting was to be done and all the glitches and so on and so forth were to be rectified. Our dancers were wearing red and white *saree* and our boys were wearing just a ready made *dhoti*. I had to wear a *dhoti* which had been coloured and designed to look like tiger's skin. A toy snake was wound around my neck and several artificial necklaces of *rudraksh* with a blue paint over my entire body completed my look as lord *shiva*. I just wished that no one should have found about my guise. It was embarrassing, firstly because I didn't had the body to flaunt as I was thin as a stick. Secondly, I prayed that aishani shouldn't recognise me.

Our team settled at the backstage and we were motivating each other, and trying to boost confidence within ourselves. My eyes were searching for aishani. I had seen her house members in the classroom adjacent to the stage. They were going to perform *bharatnatyam*. Aishani was nowhere or maybe she must be lost in between her housemates who must be asking for last minute help. Thank goodness! Before she will notice, I would have changed into the school uniform! Ours was the first performance, then *petals* and so on. There was a kind of a bitter sweet relationship with me and the stage. I always had the desire to be on the stage and speak and to be someone whom the audience will hear in silence. Whose words will create an impact in the mind and the soul of the listener. Four years ago, I had got the opportunity but if I am right, then I can just say that I lost the opportunity a bit too easily.

* * * * *

FOUR

I *used to see the news channels with my father. He always insisted on showing me the debates which the politicians as well as the analysts used to have on their news channels. At first instance, I hated these channels and would shout at my father for changing my cartoon, but after certain time, I started to look at them with a little more seriousness, with a little more reasoning. I even started analysing a person on his viewpoints and started to discuss that with my father. Certain things every Indian family know that politics is more of a festival rather than just a term dealing with the administration of the country. It is one of the rarest things which connects india and has the capability to connect india on a cup of tea in a local tea stall with the expensive cafeterias of the country. And in all of this, even a small kid of thirteen starts forming his opinions about a particular person or the party. I was not interested in the politics that time but the way in which some politicians used to conduct themselves. Some would speak in gentle tones all the times and some would try to silent the others by speaking loudly and aggressively. And some used to modulate their voices from anger to a forceful plead and then back to anger and so on. Looking up at the mirror, I used to mimic the person's facial expressions and would imitate the words used by him. That year, it was announced that even the middle school will hold its debate competition. That was it. That was my chance.*

The mimicry helped me in defeating some of the competitors of my own house who had showed interest in the debate. It was easier than I had thought.

Then came the debate day, we were given the topic an hour before the commencement of the debate and we had to prepare it. I had no idea about preparing a debate. I had never prepared it. I did what I could do best, write an essay and then speak from it. First speakers are always listened more intently than the coming ones. I was the first speaker of the day. The topic was, "can money buy happiness?" I went up to the podium. The crowd started murmuring. I got nervous. I had to speak in favour of the motion. "ladies and gentlemen, the topic on fire today is....can money buy happiness and I will speak for the motion." The beginning was good. I had spoken it loudly and clearly. But, as I had written more of an essay and less of a debate. I had to keep looking at the paper to see my next argument. I saw the judge turning uninterested. I really tried hard to speak without looking at the paper and tried to speak as confidently as I could. In the end, I stammered a couple of times and ended my argument in the middle of a sentence. "and I would like to say that.... Thank you very much." Well, that was it. My house was disqualified from that debate, the audience laughed and booed. I couldn't face my house teachers and from that day on, I started to live an even more introvert kind of a life. I started enjoying oblivion.

Sometimes I would circle the whole playground during recess, sometimes wander around the corridors, sometimes, going to the older classrooms, talking with myself, or with the boy from the past who would stand before me, wearing grey halves and light blue shirt, looking at me and wondering what he had become in the future.

The debate never happened again for me and I became a part of the audience. An audience whose job was to applause. An audience which was a crowd of different faces but same characteristic, which was- they all were an unknown entity. After four years, I was coming back.

* * * * *

FIVE

We performed well. Our dancers gave their best while I just sat and smiled at the audience. The response from the audience was good. They had enjoyed the dance. They had giggled at my entry. I heard them giggling and murmuring. It made me nervous and my knees felt weak. Not again, not again. I closed my eyes and sat. that had helped.

I rushed to the green room, washed my make up and made myself presentable again like a school child. I had wanted to see the *petals* house's performance but I was not able to. They must have done good, I thought. I imagined aishani leading the stage and the audience who must have been mesmerized by the performance. I came out of the green room only after *leaves* had performed. All the performances were done and the audience were waiting for the results. To fleet the time, our school choir was singing some retro songs. The participants looked nervous and eager. My eyes were looking for aishani.

She was standing at the back of the auditorium looking at the sun. "aishani?" she looked at me. "how powerful is the sun! isn't it? Millions of kilometres away and yet it can give us so much heat. I want to be like a sun arav." Everytime I tried to understand her, she would force me to change the perspective about her, she was a mystery, still far away from being understood. "aishani, you will be a star one day, I can see it in your eyes, you will inspire many." She smiled, "come on, let's go back, let's see if I have won or you have lost." She winked.

We stood with our team members, eagerly waiting. Our principle congratulated all of us and the teachers who had choreographed the steps. We came second. The principle said- "where is the *shivji*" I was embarrassed to go. "come up quickly arav, your teacher has told me, quickly." I went up and had a photograph. I don't know about getting the things we want but we definitely get those things which we run away from. I was trying to hide my identity from aishani but now, every student of the school knew about the *shivji.*

Petals obviously were declared the winners. They were good. Aishani was the best. All of them went up, and enjoyed their victory moment. I was happy to see aishani smiling, a smile for which she had worked hard.

"you never told me that you had to enact *shivji.*" though, she said it earnestly, yet I felt a sense of sarcasm in it. "can we talk about something else, rather than this "why-you-did-this?" conversations and why-you-did-that conversations? I am happy that you won, but don't ask about my decisions, okay?" I had said this rather rudely. I could see her face turning red. She was about to cry. I agree, I had spoken it harshly, like real harshly, with all the puns and metaphors added. "that was very rude of arav, like, seriously, that was so rude." And she started to sob. The school was over and we had decided to go home together. Her house was near the cinema hall, little ahead of my residence. "don't cry aishani, I am sorry." She started to cry more, she cried silently, and sat on the bench and put her head down. "aishani?" "no, don't talk to me." "aishani?" I tried being more sweet. "no, no no." anger had gone. She was playing a game now. I sat next to her. "okay. If this is it, then I will sit next to you and see your small nose turn red like a cherry." She glimpsed at me. "no, it wont turn red, my nose leaks and will put my running nose on your trouser." And she tried to do that. "that's disgusting." And she laughed. "the next time you make me cry, I will make sure that I soil your trousers or your shirt for that matter." I wondered if our friendship would be that long to make her cry once again.

When we are attracted towards someone, we ignore their bad qualities, and we only look at their positive qualities. In short, we start day dreaming about our love, and our love looks perfect and faultless. We start believing that we have found our infinity. That this all we always ever had wanted.

"hey aishani, can you come up. Get as soon as you can, we will be reading a new one today." Some of my school friends had created this group called *"readers and co."* where everytime, an individual would read out an entire novel with full conviction and emotion." Aishani herself was a book enthusiast and when she had heard about this club, she had become really excited. "this will be so lovely, so much to learn and enjoy." She had taken quite an interest in it and had read three books since our club's inception. Alok, aniket, sarang were the fellow members of the club.

All of them being my classmates and all of them being book lovers. Sarang had a big collection of e-books and he would tell us through them while the rest were paperback lovers.

We were meeting on a Wednesday. My house was the club centre. We all had gathered around and today it was my turn to recite a novel. "which one should I recite guys?" I asked while searching the book shelf. I had autobiographies, some scientific stuff and drama as well. The only genre which was untouched was romance. "lets read some romantic one's arav for a change." Alok joked. "I don't have any romantic ones if you ask." "don't worry, I have." Aishani had brought *ps-I love you* with herself. "you have cornered him aishani. Now he will have to read this." Everyone laughed.

"Ya, Ya, whatever, aniket. I hate you for this." We chuckled.

I began reading the book. It was about a wife whose husband had died due to a tumour at a very young age. The husband, had written ten short messages for her which she had to follow. Every message had to be opened during a particular month. The book seemed interesting and I read hundred pages in two hours. Since the book had some really emotional moments, I saw tears in the eyes of alok and aishani. Aniket was amazed and sarthak was perplexed with the book. We decided to finish this book by tomorrow. We hated losing momentum while completing a book. It was nearly seven when aishani said her good bye. Mummy liked aishani's nature. During one of her visits, she also had told her how to make *thepla*, a very famous dish of gujarat. "mummy, she is the master of all trades." "and what are you mr arav, a slave of all trades." Mummy's replies were always instant. She laughed on them.

"it's a nice book, this." I said to her at my gate, she was now on the road. "yes, it is, I can relate to the character, I can feel the love between them. It feels so divine to just think about two imaginary lovers who are just inside some two hundred pages and then they are gone and they just remain inside our heart." Her thinking was deep and her eyes were deeper. They used to shine brightly, as if expecting a brighter answer. I used to try to be as good as possible. "I think, they are real, I mean, there must be two people like them in this world of seven billion people, and I think that, these books become a kind of a tribute to those unnamed lovers who are out their and are creating love stories which, I think, will get published, sooner or later by someone. Someone will tell it…" I stopped to see aishani staring at me. She was looking spellbound. "what did you just say!"

"What do you mean?"

"I mean, what did you just say! It ripped my heart. God! It was so deep. So very deep. The romance book is playing with your heart *haa?*" she teased.

"and how does it affect you Ms aishani?" "hey! Retaliating back with a question is not fair." "come on! Don't tell me that you are a no-love-story kind of a girl." "I don't know, I am confused about this love thing and does it happens."

"I will give you a complete day to think about the answer. Time starts now. Bye and get lost." I pushed her jokingly and she went away.

Going to the school had become a kind of an excuse to meet her. I tried to concentrate on my studies as much as i could. The initial ten minutes of the class were spent in serious studies and after it, her voice would loom around the my head and I would ultimately loose concentration. That day was no less. I was wondering about what she would say about the book when my English teacher saw me, daydreaming, looking outside the class. Maam swarnika never liked me, and she got a chance to brandish that duster on me, which was her favourite weapon. "arav, I believe that you wont mind if we go for a lovely walk to the principle's office?" that day had finally come. That day, after so many dodging had finally come when I would get a warning letter for the first time. "maam, this child is a menace. He never completes my assignment, never answers the questions which I ask him in the class and he sits in the corner."

I never retaliated. The best way to handle the situation is to bow down, and wait till you are said to get out and get the letter from the office which is to be signed by the parent. I had promised mummy to get a letter from the school, which would tell about my excellence. Except that 'excellence', the dream had come true. I met aishani at the recess and showed her the letter. "you are making a good progress arav, keep it up. When is the next letter scheduled for?" "you know *naa* that I don't like this teacher, if she is a rabbit, then I am a tortoise, if she is a sun, then I am the moon, if she is Shakespeare, then I am the reader of the twenty-first century, we would never gel."

"okay cheer up! come on, don't make a gloomy face, lets go to the junior block before the recess gets over."

The junior block would always cure my anxiety. I had told aishani about it. This was our second tour in the block. Last time, I had shown her my third class, where I was scolded badly and was punished in the class. I cried in front of everybody. "you are such an emotional fool arav, really.

You should control it." Its not that I had never tried, its just that, there are two things which always takes the better of one will's to not cry- first being nostalgia and second, humiliation.

"this was where, my sixth class was. That time, pen fights had become a big craze and we would play with all sorts of pens, some would combine two pens with an elastic band. We would fight on the teachers desk because it was the best arena for big matches which had more than five or six players." She chuckled. "as a matter of fact, I become friends with alok, aniket and sarthak during these fights. Isn't it amusing?" "yea, it is."

I felt an impulse throughout my body. Aishani was staring at me, smiling, a different kind of a smile, it felt different, it felt passionate. Her eyes ripped my heart. A silence prevailed. I turned my head in the opposite side. My knees felt weak. I smiled and said "damn!" in a very low voice. She, too must be feeling shy. "let's go back to our classes, will catch you later, bye." And we hurriedly went back in our classes.

"adrenaline is an emergency hormone which is secreted during the time of fright or fight." Our bio teacher, Mrs. Avasthi said. Her eyes were frightening me and I was high on adrenaline. Despite the fright, I wanted to see her as soon as the time would allow.

School gave over at two and we met near the stage. Nothing, I mean, nothing looked normal like before. We were not able to face each other. I was feeling shy of saying anything and her head was low. Forget about a "hi", we ran to our homes.

The evening had set over the doon valley. You could see the clouds slowly coming on Mussoorie. It would probably rain in there and maybe some parts of rajpur road as well. The guys were to come at five. "hey alok!" I called alok at half past four. "yes buddy, half and hour later, I will be at your house." "no, no, no. that's why I am calling you. Listen, there is a change of plan. Mummy has to get some groceries from the supermarket and I have to go. There are no excuses about that. That's why I am calling you. Sorry alok." "that's unfortunate man, just wanted to complete that book, it gets on my nerves, you know, an incomplete book." "I understand that, we will complete it next week, I promise."

the same kind of calls were made with each of the boys. Let aishani come and then we would see why such awkward incidents had happened during the day. Would she come? I had told everyone that I had told aishani that today there would be no reading sessions. I had taken outmost care. I was looking at the road. Waiting for her. With questions in my mind and doubts in my heart. Precisely at five, a girl in red top and blue denims approached my house. She was coming.

"hey aishani! good to see you again."

"good to see you too arav."

"let's go inside."

"okay, as you say."

Aishani had thought the room to be bustling with noises but today it was quiet. "where are the boys?" she asked. "they had said that they were going kempty falls so they wont be joining us today." How wonderfully I had lied. Without a drop of hesitation.

"oh, that's unfortunate, I wanted to complete this book today."

"I know, but, never mind, maybe next week."

Mummy came to the room, with coffee. "where are the others?" she asked. "they have gone to the kempty falls. And we are marooned." Aishani smiled. "its bad that they haven't come but you two can go outside, it's a nice evening." That's what I wanted, I thought, my smile widening more and more. Things were falling into places automatically now, with hardly any efforts. "that's a good idea mummy, thank you." I said with the biggest smile I could. "shall we?" I asked aishani. She looked a bit hesitant. I could see that. Her face had turned red and an uncomfortable silence had followed. Each passing second was difficult. Its very difficult to keep your thoughts straight when your immediate future prospects are at stake. "say yes! Please please please." I kept muttering inside. "lets go." A smile curled across my lips. I closed the gate and off we went. Vasant vihar stood in front of us.

* * * * *

SIX

Vasant vihar was a jogger's delight. Trees on both sides and minimal traffic on the roads had attracted all the fitness freaks of the city. I didn't care if you ask about them.

The thing with a high school romance in india is that its not even bad but considered that the child has gone out from the parent's hand and will definitely go into oblivion. And if a relative spots you walking together with a girl, then it's the end of your life. Leave aside the relatives, even the passer bys will get something to gossip and chit chat in their free time for atleast a week. So, naturally, it was an awkward situation but the courage which I had found to ask her for this wont come again and so I decide to give it a risk. Maybe tomorrow wont give me this happiness. Maybe tomorrow, aishani will not remain in my life. A silence had prevailed for five minutes since we had walked. I needed to break it. Somehow, a conversation needed to be started. "see them." I said, looking at her, pointing towards pedestrians. "they must have decided to go for an evening walk not because they like it, but because they had to show themselves as health conscious people. I guarantee that they had *pakoda* just before coming." Aishani laughed to that. "that was a very keen observation Mr Sharma. Yes, you are right. Dieting is such a massive thing. Everyone wants to lose weight. Alas! No one achieves it. I don't think that losing weight makes a person more beautiful. I am good as I am." She smiled. "you are beautiful aishani." Another awkward silence. That just came out involuntarily. "ass! Stupid!" I cursed myself. Aishani and I reached the citizen's park. We sat on one of the benches. The place had some children and one or two elderlies. "so, Mr Sharma, I am curious as to know why we are here, sitting on a bench in a park?" she asked, raising her eyebrows. She asked mischievously. "there is nothing in this world which can make me answer that question." I replied with equal mischief. She was curious, that was clearly evident. She wanted to know and I wanted to tell. But, but, but I stopped. Time was not right and the mood was not set. *Let it drip subtly,* I said, composing myself. "listen. I wanted to ask you have some good romantic books. I love it when they love." "yeah sure, why not. I don't have them but I will arrange it for you. Sun had almost set, leaving a golden speck. "its so usual but it is beautiful as ever." "yes it is." Aishani was looking at me. A peculiar look. She looked happy but she was not smiling. Maybe she was confused herself. The park had silenced. Everyone had left, except us. "lets go home now." She spoke softly. "lets go, sure." The evening had went good. I was content. We walked silently. There was hardly anything more to talk about. Not that I wasn't thinking about starting a topic, but I somehow felt that moments of silence are equally important. Our movements were in sync. We took each step together. It was amusing to see that. Our hands touched each other. Her hand was cold. "your hands are so cold aishani." "and your hands are warm." "isn't it a perfect combination. Hot and cold mix together, giving stability." It sounded pleasing. It had the necessary warmth to keep me going, and asking- "what was it today?" "what do you mean?" she knew exactly what I meant, but it's the thing with girls, they want to hear from someone else. I had decided that I will answer her out, no matter what. "I know that you know that. And there is no way by which you are going to escape this situation. You have to answer and answer it loud and clear." I was firm, yet polite. She stared at me. I knew that "getting embarrassed" and things like that but still I needed an answer because that thing was going constantly in my mind for ten hours now. We were walking slower than before. Just to keep the momentum, we had not stopped, and we had crossed my house once, and were just circling the area. "I felt attached with you. And not that type of attachment but that *wala* attachment." Her face was red. Under the halogen streetlamp, we stopped. There was no soul on the road. All the souls were inside these decorated wallpapers, Except us. This was the first time, anything like that had happened with me, so naturally I was shaking. She was looking down, the typical aishani pose. I held her hand-"I don't know how you have become this important to me. I used to think of myself as a loner but you have shared this loneliness. I laugh at my friends when they show me those conversations with their girlfriends. I thought it was kiddish. maybe its not. When you get attached to someone, you are bound to be a little kiddish. Isn't it?" she was looking at me with a warm smile. "yes arav. Yes." She was smiling. I gently gave her a side hug for a couple of seconds. It was an intimate moment. Who said that kisses are intimate? He must have never hugged properly otherwise he would have known the intimacy and the gush of emotion which sweeps across a hug.

. . . .

"what? Was there anything to laugh about?" supriya was rolling out on the grass. "hot and cold mix together giving stability!" and she kept on laughing, repeating these words. "is it so funny? Isn't it? Its not easy to confess. That too face to face. A message on messenger is way easy. Will you stop laughing?" "oh sorry sorry. This story is no doubt amusing. What happened then?" "do you really want me to continue? Its almost one. We have been here for three hours. Aunty must be worried." "no, please continue, I will tell mummy that the extra class at coaching got extended. Simple." And she did that. How curious we are to hear stories about each other! Deep down, I, myself was excited to tell her all this. All of this time, it had been too difficult to keep this secret. I had once read a quotation which said-keep your relationships secret to enjoy it to the fullest. I had kept this in my mind during the early days, then I decided to throw this thought away and tell. Supriya, as I had told before was the first listener.

. . . .

I switched on my laptop to see if she was online. She was. I decided to call her. Calling, always has an upper hand. Chats don't carry emotions with them, voice does. That's why god gave us a voice box and not pencils and papers at the beginning. It rang straightaway. Needless to say, adrenaline was already being pumped at its peak potential.

"hello?", she knew that it was me, but the hide up of a woman is better than a guise of Sherlock holmes. You cant predict her face to face, leave about a mobile. "aishani, its arav." I was barely speaking. It was a relatively new feeling for me. I didn't have a girlfriend to talk to. Now you were not just friend. You had taken a step ahead. "I will meet you tomorrow at school, right after the morning assembly." I agreed to it. The next set of questions were a little over the top dramatic ones like how was the dinner and what was there in the dessert and if some family member had sneezed during the dinner, then was he okay or not. A sudden feeling of responsibility had surged. Her family members were also my family members and vice versa. We hung up soon after saying goodnights to each other. That was a first in my life. I felt thrilled about it. An ordinary goodnight had the potential to keep you awake. I barely slept that night. The goodnight had an overwhelming euphoric effect.

Vincent academy had never looked this beautiful in all of the twelve years. I was little early. The school gates had just opened and I sat on the staircase of the stage. There was just me and one fourth grade staff, sweeping the auditorium. Another of the staff was opening the classrooms. Time had slowed, like it always did with those who were waiting. Classes opened and after putting my bag at the front bench, I came back. Few students had come. There I saw aishani, getting in her class. She had arrived early. I waited for her to come out of the class. She saw me. I pointed towards the back stage. That was a confined place, and a safer one, because though it was an open area, it was not visible from three sides and secondly, it was mainly used for keeping old furniture of the school.

None of us spoke. There was quietness. I had planned that I would say this and that but it didn't come out. There was much to say but nothing to express. I had tonnes of things to talk about, but I was smiling and mumbling. Minor hiccups at the beginning, I thought. When you get embarrassed at your own self. The bell rang. We looked at each other's face. Can't you say something? Before going to our houses, we promised to meet during the recess.

* * * * *

It's winter and there is no one around except the large canopies.

The growth of these trees is huge. I am unable to walk in the snow covered pathway. "why am I here?" I keep asking myself. I don't even know how I had come here. Suddenly, a sound of laughter erupts through the chilled silence of the forest. I look everywhere but I don't see a soul.

"looking for me?" someone said it. It was just a whisper but I had heard it. Yet there was nobody in sight.

"who is there?" I finally said. The silence was terrifying me.

"you were looking for me, all the time. And now you have found me."

"why would I look for you?"

"everyone looks for me, everyone searches for me."

"show me yourself. Why are you hiding?"

"I am hiding because it is not the right time for me to show up. I hope to see you soon."

And she disappeared.

Oh! These dreams! These wintery dreams!

* * * * *

SEVEN

I always paid attention to what our principle use to say during the morning assembly. But not today, not at all. I tried peeping from house to see her. The student standing behind me must have given me a "certified pervert award" for my hawk eye analysis. The worse thing was that I didn't see her. Our house was sent first to the classrooms. So there was no chance of meeting. Recess, three hours to go, I sighed.

"what do you think of love at first sight?" our English teacher was explaining Romeo and Juliet. I smiled. What a perfect way to start today's day. "Is it even possible? Who wants to show his or her opinion?" I raised my hand proudly. Every one stared at me. I know what they must have thought. Love and arav? Poles apart. No chance at all. They had forgot this thing- unlike poles attract each other. "love can happen at first sight. I mean, if you don't connect at the first instant, then how will you connect the second or the third time. Its not a gas lighter which if it works the second time or third time, it will burn the flame. It has to work at the very first instance." Everyone listened to it attentively.

Teacher was impressed. "that's a nice way to look at it. Are you in love or something?" my face reddened. "no, no. I am not." And I laughed embarrassingly. Romeo and Juliet had fuelled my eagerness to meet aishani. Still there were three classes to go. And we had double periods of mathematics. Enough maths to wash out romance from your brains. "madam, I need to go to the washroom." She looked at me angrily, "school has just started and you want to go to the washroom? Shame on you. Go." Never I had been retorted this badly. It was humiliating. But I kept my head down and went out. Who wanted to go to the washroom? No one. I had to meet aishani. I came hurriedly downstairs and saw her class. She was sitting near the window. She was looking outside the class, hardly interested in the subject. I laughed at it. Stupid girl! "sir, may I come in?" I entered aishani's class. i went straight to the teacher without looking at the students. "what is the matter?" the teacher asked. "aishani is being called by the dance teacher." Aishani was surprised. "right now?" she asked me.

"yes. Right now."

She came out of the classroom.

"why is she calling me?"

"I don't know. We will figure it out."

I deliberately took the longest way, through the junior block. We reached the dance room. There was no one. "where is madam?" she asked. "who? I don't know. She hadn't called you either." Her eyebrows widened. "then?" "I chalked this up." She laughed. "you are so stupid arav. We would have met in the recess." "I know that, but still, you know." "you know what?" "don't tease me." I punched her playfully on the face. "I know you boys, you just want to bunk. You all are the same." "what? Where does this thing come from?" I was happy that our usual nonsense fight had come back. "what are you two doing over here?" madam shubhika, our dance teacher had come. "we were just going back from the water cooler." We hurriedly walked away. "we should get back to the classroom. The last thing I want from the school is a warning letter." I took the different staircase and ran to my class room. "enjoyed the walk?" madam remarked. I smiled shamefully and went to my seat and waited for the recess. "shameless creature", she must have said. I didn't listen.

After three longest hours of my life, we met during the recess. "let's go to the back field." Canteen would be the worst place to go. Everyone would just hop into our food stuff and random jokes would be cracked, which would be so pathetic that you would start laughing on the pathetic-ness of the joke. Elephant and ant jokes would be re-incarnated and dubbed into a more adult by making a reference about sex. And if that didn't work, we always had a cuss word to entertain.

I was not feeling hungry at all. Saliva had completely dried up and my stomach felt full. I had opened my lunchbox, only to see a plain *parantha* rolled with a pickle. That was enough. I surrendered.

We sat in the backfield. It was an awkward situation. No senior would sit in the backfield surrounded by kids on all sides. But when cupid strikes, you hardly think, isn't it?

She was quietly eating her lunch and I had nothing to do except looking at her and sometimes left and right. She was eating consciously because she knew where we were.

"why aren't you eating?" she asked.

"not hungry." "why, what happened?"

"I don't know." Was it normal to not get hungry immediately after getting in a relationship? It was true for me, though.

We hardly spoke more than four sentences but the silence was not discomforting. When silence speak more than words, there is no need of words.

* * * * *

At three in the afternoon, I logged in to my messenger. She was online.

Arav: how was the day?

Aish_pearl: it was boring arav, I don't like maths and there were two periods of it today. Need a sleep.

Arav: happens with me all the time.

Aish_pearl: really? I used to think about you as big nerd guy, happily scribbling notes. I mean, I was very afraid to talk to you. You looked so serious everytime. You still look that ways though.

Arav: I don't want people to see my real self.

Aish_pearl: real self? What's that supposed to mean?

Arav: I am a very sentimental person. I cry when people die in movies or when some emotional music kicks in.

Aish_pearl: seriously! LMAO! This is another level of sentimental-ness. By the way, which movies? I will make sure that you watch them with me. I will then record your reaction.

Arav: that's so mean of you, to see your boyfriend cry.

That was the first time I had called myself her boyfriend. I felt a tickle in my stomach. How much childish anyone would say, but I had this wish to be called a boyfriend and to be teased this way.

Aish_pearl: haha! See my real self and be scared.

Arav: Never going to get scared from you or your honest side. It is better to be stabbed from front than from the back.

Aish_pearl: oh my god! Why you take things so seriously arav? I was just kidding. I usually do these kinds of jokes with my friends.

Arav: It's not your fault. Actually, even after so many years, I have not been able to accustom myself with this humour.

Aish_pearl: from which planet have you come from who don't laugh at these jokes arav?

Arav: not a different planet but from a different environment. Lot of hardships has made me a sad person. You know that thing.

Aish_pearl: I remember those conversations. They brought me closer to you.

Arav: indeed aishani, indeed.

* * * * *

I stopped my story. It was nearly four now. we had been there since ten.

"why have you stopped?" supriya asked me. She had been so much interested in this that she had forgotten that It was nearly four. "please tell me." She was keenly looking at my face, expecting an approval. "No, I won't tell anymore because its really late now. she looked at me with pleading eyes but I didn't move. "go home now. it's late."

"I won't forgive you for not telling me. Bye."

"I was thinking to tell you more next Sunday but, anyways, bye."

She looked so happy after that. "I will be there at ten for sure."

She hurriedly made her exit from the temple. I lied down on the grass, thinking about her. I had called aishani that day and had told that I will disclose about our relationship to supriya. No one had the slightest idea about us. We had such an amazing understanding that we looked more like best friends.

"Supriya is a very good friend. It will be okay if you tell her about us. She might become an important negotiator during our fights."

aishani had said the night before.

"I will not fight with you or will try to not fight with you."

"oh really? We'll see Mr. Sharma." I loved the way she teased.

* * * * *

"I wish you could see her amazement aishani. She was so shocked." I was telling aishani about the things which had happened today. She was eagerly waiting for my call.

She giggled- "obviously she must have got a shock. She couldn't have imagined us together."

"but we are together. Very much together. Just separated by two lanes and connected to each other through connections."

"arav, are you talking to someone?" mummy had woke up suddenly. It was twelve In the night. I had to cut her phone. Before she entered my room, I sprang upon the blanket and wrapped myself with it. She switched on the lights for a moment and then switched it off and moved out.

I messaged aishani-

Arav: it was a close call. It is difficult to talk on the phone. We can text.

She gave me another surprise.

Arav_aishani: isn't this something?

Arav: that's so thoughtful of you. You surely know how to make someone happy.

Arav_aishani: I know I am awesome. Anyways, how was your experience with mummy, few minutes ago?

Arav: you should try this out. Then you will know that heart can beat at the rate of ninety kilometres per hour.

Arav_aishani: I know that it can go to a hundred. I have experienced it once.

Arav: when? You never told me that?

Arav_aishani: when you confessed, it probably would have burst out. It was so scary.

Arav: the confession was equally difficult. I had no clue how I got so much of guts to say. I didn't say "I love you" though.

Arav_aishani: then say it now.

Arav: what?

Arav_aishani: don't annoy me. Please say those three magical words.

Arav: aishani.

Arav_aishani: arav, yes.

Arav: I know that I am a nerd and that I mug up everything. But you are the most important chapter I have learned by heart.

Arav_aishani: what the hell was that! ROFL!

Arav: I love you is so mainstream!

* * * * *

EIGHT

I had called up supriya at my house. I had to complete the story telling. I was more excited to tell her, than she was.

"okay bhai, from the day we left. I have waited eight complete days. It should better be in detail." Supriya gave all the instructions before proceeding.

"okay okay. I will abide by all the rules and will provide you with details most accurately."

"details? Who is speaking about details?" aishani popped up from the door. I was surprised. I looked at supriya. She was the one who had invited her.

"I mean, are there tickets available for this show?" talking about your relationship in front of your girlfriend with another person is one of the most awkward things you can face in your life.

"you guys are." I gave a sigh.

"Mr. Sharma, tell us about your love story!" they said together.

"I am going to kill you two. You two will not laugh." Aishani started giggling, "and especially you won't" I narrowed my eyes towards aishani. They all became quiet. How excitedly aishani looked at me! "I don't know why I am I doing this." Everybody laughed. "you should have thought about it before." Aishani winked.

* * * * *

Exams were to begin from the mid of august and we had not studied much. There is an external stimulus which stops you from studying. That external stimulus is a mobile phone. And though we tried to prove the innocence of the mobile phone in front of parents, it had always been proved 'guilty.'

It required extra humane efforts to let go off your mobile phone.

"I have not studied anything arav! What is going to happen? I have done the biggest mistake of my life by taking up science. I shouldn't have taken it up."

"stop thinking useless things. Exams are beginning in two days and what you have to do is organize yourself."

"how much have you studied arav?"

"I tried to complete my syllabus but was not able to do. I will have to organize myself, then it will be good, I guess."

"please help me. I don't want to fail." "I won't let you fail. Should you find yourself free, come at my house anytime you want and we will sort the mess out. I have some previous year papers which would help you a lot in understanding the weight age of the chapters. Don't worry. I am here."

She came to my house within an hour. In her typical way, she said- "I found myself free."

"how much have you revised?" I asked her. She looked dazed and confused. I understood the situation. She hasn't studied at all.

"umm, a little maybe." her eyes twinkled. I was trying to be very serious, but the expression of her face was making me smile all the time.

"what are you looking at?" she had not come to study but talk, but I was ignoring her questions and searching for the previous year questions.

"here, these are of physics and chemistry. And let me find English. English is very important. You have to score good in that." She nodded in agreement.

"I will fail this time. I am confident about this." "you will pass, don't worry. Just study well and don't assume that you are going to fail."

She had done some of the basic chapters only and that were mostly irrelevant. Nothing would be coming from them, and all the important ones she had skipped.

"aishani." I said in a very calm and composed manner. "why haven't you done these chapters?"

"they were too difficult. I couldn't do." I smacked my forehead in shock. "you should have asked from someone. now what will happen?"

"I will fail." There she went again.

The next thirty minutes I told her what all to do in all the subjects and counseling her that she will not fail.

"aishani, its getting late. Mummy must be waiting." Mummy had just came upstairs. That was the signal for her to leave.

"yes aunty. I was just going. thank you arav. That will surely help."

After she was gone, mummy came to my room. "now you study. This is the board year. No compromises are to be made." I had to nod in a positive.

* * * * *

We met in the school, before the first exam. "we have to make an agreement." She said to me.

"what sort of agreement?" I was puzzled with this new agreement.

"first, we will only call each other at night and if that's not possible, we will message." That was fair enough. She was getting serious about exams and that was the only thing which I had concern about.

"secondly, between the exam, we will not meet in the park at all.

"that's harsh but if that's going to improve your marks, then why not."

"And the third is, we will go to George Everest on the last day of the exam." She gave a big smile. That was not a clause. It was more of a reward.

"agreed." You have to leave some things behind in order to get something in the future.

* * * * *

The first exam was English and it went off well. This subject always helped me in gaining the moral boost. It could also be said that, after reading so much of Shakespeare's works, I had become a romantic, which had made me a little more vulnerable to all these emotions. I was more permeable to love than I ever was.

Arav: are you there?

I had messaged aishani at night. The next day was a study gap for chemistry and economics. The reply came instantaneously.

Arav_aishani: yes! I am there. How was your exam?

Arav: it went good. Hoping that chemistry is the same. How was yours?

Arav_aishani: it was better than I had expected. All thanks to those question papers which helped a lot. I owe it to you.

Arav: you don't need to mention it. Always and anything for you.

Arav_aishani: hmm

Arav: what happened? A "hmm" from you? OMG!

Arav_aishani: I am not perfect for you arav. I am not the choice.

I had heard this sentence many times from my classmates. I used to say to them- "why have you come in a relationship in which the person doesn't have confidence about their own self?" Now I was at the same crossroad.

This question popped up suddenly. My heart skipped a beat. My mind had no readymade solutions.

She was waiting for the answer and I was taking a lot of time.

Arav: its not like that.

Arav_aishani: if it was not like that, then why did you take so much time?

The situation was getting bad.

Arav_aishani: it's because, even you have a doubt. Isn't it?

Arav: now listen up. I am not a judge in a reality show who is there to judge contestants and select the candidates who are better than the rest. I only wanted a person who could understand me. And you fit that criterion more than I could bargain for. So, you never ever say that again.

Arav_aishani: I thought that maybe my too much indulgence in your life was creating problem for you.

Arav: it's ridiculous to even think that ways. Let me tell you what has happened after you have come in my life. I have started caring. I have started understanding emotions. I have started valuing suggestions. And all of this is because of you.

Arav_aishani: have I?

Arav: more than you can imagine. Now go and study for the next exam. And let me study too.

Arav_aishani: yes, bye.

She never said that she was not perfect for me again.

* * * * *

Cool winds and a cloudy weather welcomed us as we came out from the last exam. This is one good day to go to mussoorie. What a perfect timing!

Aishani came out a little late from the exam hall.

"all set?" I asked her.

"I think, yes. Let's go."

"I drive a little slow, so don't expect speed and thrills." I joked. She chuckled.

"where are you guys heading?" supriya popped out from nowhere.

But I accelerated the scooty that very moment. "enjoy the loneliness supriya!" "get lost. I am angry with you." She screamed. We laughed as we saw her face through the rear view mirror.

"finally, arav, after so many days, we are together for more than fifteen minutes." She said happily.

"I know. Even I feel the same. These exams test a lot of things, just not your knowledge, isn't it."

"should we go straightaway to George everest or some other place first?" I had asked because I wanted to enjoy the whole day with her.

"let's go to sahastradhara first. I went there a long time ago. I have heard that the place has changed a lot, so it will be quite an experience."

That's what I wanted to hear. "alright, next stop sahastradhara."

The journey was eternally peaceful to sahastradhara. There were hardly any honkers, absolutely no potholes and aishani, with whom I could talk about anything in this world. Her gossips never end. They were a delight to listen to. The way she explained was too amusing to ignore.

I had very little to say in these because I had hardly any friends and all, who were there, never gossiped about anything else than computer games and rock music.

Sahastradhara, as the name suggests has numerous water channels, trickling down the mountains. The water has it's medicinal use in treating skin diseases. Hence, you could always see people with skin disorders taking a dip in the sulfur water. There was a cable car which went up to the *sai baba temple*. Aishani looked super excited to see all of this.

"let's go up first, please." She requested like an innocent child of seven.

We went up the cable car and saw that, there were many more things other than the temple. There was a small trekking camp, and a food court and a big spacious lawn.

"isn't this beautiful?" the entire area of Sahastradhara was visible. Everywhere, it was just streams of water, getting collected and ultimately forming a river.

It was mesmerizing to watch. "let's go down. We have lots to do today."

"oh yes! Let's go."

The water was super cold. It felt like ice but in the liquid form.

Even a splash was bone chilling. Aishani was having a time of her life. she was spilling water all over my body. "easy easy aishani. My god! What has happened to you?" she was so full of energy.

"just stress relieving. I am so much madness!" I got shocked to see this shade of her. This shade suited her better.

"aishani, can we go now? or you want to stay here?" I was loving the madness. It was unadulterated. It had nothing hideous about it. Madness could be fun too, I realized that day.

"okay love, let's go. I am done." She finally said after splashing another liter of water on me.

It had grown cold. Black clouds covered most of the skies and sun had hid itself under the blanket of these monstrous clouds which meant rain any moment. It was still afternoon but it had grown completely dark when we reached barlowganj.

"I am feeling cold." That ice cold water had started showing effects. Aishani had sneezed twice but she was saying that she was fine.

The entire mussoorie- dehradun road is a delight. Throughout the way, at the top, you can see the queen of hills waiting for you and at the bottom; you could see the entire DOON valley. Today was even better. The entire valley was covered with clouds.

"we are above the clouds arav. It looks beautiful. There! Look. I can touch these clouds." Aishani was trying to touch smoky clouds which had come as low as the scooty's headlamps.

The road after barlowganj was unmetalled. It was a bumpy twenty minute journey to the George everest. This place was the residence of the first general of the archaeological survey of India, Sir George Everest. The house was mostly in shambles. But the main attraction was the scenic beauty. But today, it was mostly clouds. Nothing was visible and the temperature had fallen low very low. After seeing the ruins of the house, we came outside. the clouds were settling heavily over the place. It would surely rain.

"what do we do?" I asked her. She was the one who had said about coming here before the exams.

"I had thought that it will be fun. "she looked disappointed. "I should never have said about coming here."

I never understood why she used to take all the blame on herself everytime.

"Let's go. I have a wonderful place to show you." The first drops of rain had started to fall on us. We had to hurry.

It started raining torrentially. Big rain drops fell on our clothes. We were drenched within minutes. I was finding it difficult to drive. The visibility had reduced. I was searching for a shack or a restaurant. There were none on that road.

We found a small eatery at barlowganj. The rain had become more torrential.

Aishani was looking at the rain. "It doesn't seem like ending any time sooner." I said to her. She turned around and nodded.

The small eatery had lots of bakery products. An old uncle was at the counter. I smiled at him. He smiled back.

"would you have something to eat?" he asked politely.

"what all do you have sir?" I asked him. Aishani came to the counter.

"apple pies is my forte. Please try that." That sounded so delicious that saliva dripped from my mouth. He laughed heartily. "it happens, all the time. They are a real treat for your taste buds." The baker uncle was super confident about his pies.

"let's see what he brings. We sat on the only two chairs available to sit in the shop.

"here you are children, apple pie." That pie looked sober. Nothing that great in the appearance. But the taste was amazing. The smell of red wine in the pie gave it a characteristic fragrance.

"apple pie tastes best with…" he paused for a moment and then showed a big red bottle. "grapewine."

We looked at each other. "no, thankyou uncle, we would just have the apple pie and be gone."

"yes uncle, please, no." Aishani replied with a laugh. "we are not adults."

He looked at us and smiled, "that's good to hear that some children don't pretend themselves as adults. God bless, children."

Rain had reduced but had still not stopped. Nevertheless, we decided to make our way back.

"that was such an amazing trip." Aishani had absolutely loved it. "but, mummy will kill me for coming back this late." "we are just fours behind our schedule, no need to worry." I giggled.

"very funny no? okay, I am going in. please pray that I am not killed." She ran inside.

The rain of summer will connect us divine
Which we wanted to, always.
I loved her so much that I couldn't explain.
Sometimes in my dreams, I say to you-
"aishani, I love you so much."
"what happened arav?"
"it's nothing. Just wanted to say this again and again."
Love the person as much as you did when you prayed so
that she could be yours.

* * * * *

"arav, aishani has come." I was still sleeping. Who comes this early on a Sunday? It was eight in the morning and I was allowed to sleep till nine.

"get up Mr. Sharma, procrastinator. Wake up." She barged into my room.

"I mean, why have you come to ruin my precious Sunday sleep?" I was still drowsy and on my bed, wrapped in a blanket.

"just move it. I have something to show you."

"you shall not be spared in hell for disturbing one's peaceful sleep. Now if you will excuse me."

"sure sure." She went out of the room, laughing.

I tried to sanitize myself as much as I could in fifteen minutes.

"which thing made you so excited that you came before the newspaper bhaiya?" the newspaper bhaiya had come though, my bad.

"I have brought this."

She showed me a handmade box, on which it was written- 'To make him cry.'

Inside it were movies. I laughed loudly.

"are you serious? You took that thing too seriously, isn't it?"

"nothing would be as good as to see you cry." she gave a devilish laugh.

"you are crazy." "I know. Don't I?"

We started our movie spree with "all or nothing." It was an emotionally moving story about a wife and her husband and the struggles they had to face in their relationship. Some parts were downright emotional.

Aishani kept a check by looking at me all the time.

"what? Why are you looking at me like that?"

"you are not crying! This was such an emotional scene!" she irritatingly said.

I laughed at this. "sorry, try again."

she played another movie, "life is beautiful." The movie was genuinely good. it was about the hardships of a couple in the world war.

She, then played 'the shawshank redemption' and boy! The narration chilled my spines. The narration about losing a friend because you, yourself want him to do well in life was heart touching.

"finally, something which made you lose a drop." I smiled at her. "I cry at the most unexpected things. You should have played this movie first, then you wouldn't have waited four hours!"

"It was more important to fleet my time with you. It was more important to see you react at the small things. It was important to put my head above your shoulders." She whispered the last line.

"and I thought you were a little crazy. You are mad." I replied

"I am madly in love with a boy of eighteen who cries at smallest of the things."

"madly?" I jokingly asked.

"madly." She confirmed with a smile.

* * * * *

Supriya stared at me as if I had told her the secret of life and death. She looked at me and then at aishani and then again at me.

"you two are so different from each other. I know that aishani is a bit shy towards strangers but with friends, she is a mess, but you are always so calm. I still can't believe this."

Aishani laughed at this. "supriya, love never waits for your order. It happens anytime, anywhere, anyplace. That's why it is so much vulnerable and that is the same reason why it is so pure. It is devoid of money and lust."

"that's why I made her my sleeping eight." I winked at aishani.

"sleeping eight?" supriya didn't know the symbol of eternity. It was more of a symbol of love than just a simple mathematical symbol. Infinity.

"infinity, my dearest sister. Infinity."

* * * * *

we three had formed a group on messenger and we would talk anything and everything on it. Supriya was the over enthusiastic one, waking us up with good morning messages and bidding us good night with some thought provoking quote lurched in the background of moon light. We had named this group as 'three musketeers.' Obviously, none of us had read that but since it sounded so good that we made it as the group name.

aishani and I still preferred the private inbox but in order to give supriya companionship, we would talk all day long. The preboards were still two weeks away and the festive season had just begun.

Our society celebrated diwali in the park. No other place was allowed to burst the crackers. I had gave up crackers some years ago and was more into sweets. At nine, we had decided to meet near the park.

'happy diwali love." Aishani whispered.

"happy diwali." I had brought a broche for her from my savings. She gifted me a wallet. The first gift we had given to each other. The others were busy in celebration, and we sneaked out on my scooty to supriya's place. The entire road was abuzz with crackers and children running here and there. Every house had been decorated with different lights. Some stopped before the others while some kept blinking. This was the festival which DOON valley enjoyed the most.

Supriya was outside her house, lighting candles. "can we help in putting up the candles?" supriya was delighted to see us. "finally! I thought you wouldn't come. Come on in. lets go the terrace and light some lamps."

Supriya had arranged the lamps in the shape of a swastika on the terrace. Every lamp was ready to be lit.

"here, take these." she gave a candle to us and we started lighting those lamps. It gave me immense peace. It was such a happy moment. Three friends, on a terrace, lighting lamps on a festival.

Aishani took a lamp and brought it to me. "we will light this together, arav."

I held her hand while she lit that lamp. "this is happiness." I said to her. "indeed." She looked around at me and smiled.

"lets capture this moment. Supriya, get a camera please. We will store this moment for ever." Supriya came with her DSLR and we clicked some really precious moments.

Coming back from her house, we didn't speak anything at all. Maybe we had ran out of topics. Maybe we didn't need a topic. Silence was lovely.

We quietly went inside the park and got involved in the celebrations. Diwali couldn't have been better.

* * * * *

Hardly a month had gone, than we were told about our preliminary exams, which were to start in the mid of November.

"again?" aishani asked in shock. Everyone was in a shock. We knew that we were to have prelims in the month of January but this additional exam was an additional burden on the already existing piles of burdens.

"I don't know how many exams I will be giving this year." I said with an air of disappointment in my voice. The exams were to be conducted in two weeks. Ample of study gaps had been given. That was good as well as bad. Good thing was that I would study thoroughly during those gaps but the bad thing was that I would not be able to go out in the park with aishani. And to make the matters worse, my mobile phone was to be taken away.

"tough times ahead." She said, patting my back. "don't worry about us."

"don't leave me." A sudden fear of losing her had crept in. was I seeing her for the last time?

"are you stupid? I am not going to leave you, And where would I go? No one is arav. I want arav only."

"and I want aishani only." I dropped her at her house.

"all the best arav. And don't worry." She went in. I stayed there till she had closed the door of her house and had signaled me to go away.

* * * * *

I didn't know how to spend my spend time during the exam days. I had nothing to do, except remembering aishani and the conversations which we used to have. Mummy shouldn't have taken my mobile phone, I always looked at her with a sorrowful face that maybe she would return it back before, but she didn't.

"I have to search for sample papers on the internet. Can I take my mobile?" I had asked her once before my physics exam.

"you have plenty of sample papers as far as I know. You have more than enough of the test papers. What you need to do is study those materials and everything will be good." Mummy's answer made it clear that she had no intentions about giving my mobile back.

I started writing poems about love and romance. They were not good at all but they provided with me satisfaction.

You become a writer when you fall in love or when you get a betrayal in love. There was no third reason.

Even when I went to school to give the exam, I searched for aishani. Maybe, I would see her going to her optional class or dance room. But I had not been able to. Once I saw supriya who was hurriedly walking to the computer laboratory with her typical 'scared for life' face. We would say a prayer before going to the exam and then sent to the exam hall. That was the routine.

* * * * *

I now knew that why the optional exam was put in the last. It always brought happiness on our faces. Firstly, because it was the easiest of the whole lot and secondly, it indicated the beginning of freedom.

There was buzzing and murmuring when we submitted the last paper to the invigilator. That happiness when you give the last exam is the purest form of happiness. Even that person smiles back at you which normally ignores you all the time.

All the conversation was mainly involving the farewell and the last days of the school and how much would they miss this place afterwards. Alok and aniket who sat behind me were discussing about the bike ride which they will go just after school.

"Can you two just stay inside your house for one day?"

"No! and by the way, we always call you for our trips but you never come. I wonder what you do in that sleepy colony of yours all day."

I laughed at this. What to tell you guys that there is someone for whom I was waiting to meet after all these days who awakes the sleepiness of that colony for me.

* * * * *

"aunty, *Namaste*. Where is aishani?" I had come in the evening of my last exam.

"how was your exams?" a generic question asked by her mother. I made a big smile and said that it was very good.

"she is upstairs. Should I bring something to eat?"

"no, thank you aunty. I am full and so will be aishani."

After so many days, I was meeting her. I was so excited. I slowly opened the door. She was reading a book at the window side.

"mummy, I will not eat anything please. I need to finish the book." She said while being deeply engrossed in the book. I entered the room quietly and closed it. I suddenly sprang on her that she screamed loudly.

"FUCK!" she screamed so loudly. I fell on the floor, laughing.

"I will kill you someday and that day is coming near." She was still shaken.

"what happened? Is everything good?" her mother asked from downstairs.

"yes mummy, everything is good. It was nothing." She stared at me for doing that. I was still laughing.

"finally, you are back." "did you missed me?" I asked.

"absolutely not. Why would I?" she said

"which book are you reading? Show me."

"why? I am reading no?"

"and you say that you don't miss me?"

She had her mobile phone in the book and she was reading the messages.

"maybe a little." She whispered.

* * * * *

Wintery dreams

Behind the canopy, she was hiding from me. I could see her clearly. "I see you." I said. "no, you can't." I ran up to her. The thick snow made It difficult to run. I could barely walk. There was no one in sight except the tall canopies.

"now I have got you?" I said to her as I stood behind her.

She turned around. She smiled. "No, my love, you have not caught me."

She disappeared suddenly. Where had she gone and how could she disappear!

"can you see me?" I heard her voice. I saw her hiding behind the other canopy.

I went to her slowly and without making any noise.

She vanished again. "what kind of a game was she playing?"

"you can't touch me. You can never touch me." Her voice echoed.

"where are you? How can you disappear? That's not possible."

All I could hear was laughs.

"you think I am showing every bit of myself to you? Am I not hiding anything? Think again."

"you will never hide anything from me. I know that."

"is it so?"

And she came near to me and went through my body and disappeared in a smoke.

I woke up. The clock ticked five.

It was the last month of the year, December.

NINE

By the time December came, there was an atmosphere of goodbyes in the school. No teacher would scold us, no teacher would give us lengthy assignments. Every junior of ours would come to us and would talk to us and tell that he would miss all of us. In return, we could say nothing except- 'We will miss you too.'

Aishani was to perform a dance for us in the farewell. She was preparing it from all her hearts.

Whenever she would reply late, I would leave a message on the messenger- "you have already bid your goodbyes?" and she would quickly reply with a big no.

"You haven't told me about your dance? Which dance form?"

"It's a secret arav. All of us have agreed to this. It's a surprise for all of you."

"it better be good."

"It will be, Mr. Sharma. It's for you, my love."

I had secured average marks in the preboards but it was okay. The paper was hailed as difficult unanimously by everyone. No one wanted to spoil their mood due to these exams. Even the re-tests were scheduled after the farewell party.

"how is it going aish?" I peeked through the window of the dance room.

"go away arav. Go go." She tried to shoo me.

"I don't think so. I won't go." I teased.

"madam, he is not going away. Such an irritating person he is." She made her face like a small baby, as if pretending that she would cry.

"arav, leave immediately. Why you always irritate her? She is so sweet. She is performing for you guys."

"okay madam. I will see you after the school." I made an angry face. Her face turned pale. Now it's my turn to enjoy, I laughingly thought.

* * * * *

"what happened?" we met in the ground, after the school got over at two. She had hurriedly come and looked worried. I was still showing that I was angry.

"arav!" she stretched it to ten syllables. I felt a tickle. I loved it when she did that. Still, I didn't melt. Not so easy this time, I glared at aishani.

"okay, I am sorry. Do I have to do sit-ups now?"

"no, its fine." I said arrogantly.

I strode forward, ignoring her. Now was the time when she would come and grab my hand and shout at me. When I turned around, I saw her running in the opposite direction, towards the back gate. I ran behind her. She took the stairs and went upstairs. Where was she going?

She then stopped in front of a classroom. I stopped behind her. This was the class which I had shown her at the beginning of our lovely journey.

"you know arav, this was the place which you showed me. Before that, it was just an ordinary classroom with desks and chairs. You put life into it. And then this place became extraordinary."

"I understand that you got connected with this place. But what happened that you came here running?"

"You know arav, I knew that you were just teasing me." Her voice broke down.

"And I know that in all these months, you tried to keep me happy all the time. I would remember you teasing me and then loving me more and more everytime. I wanted to show the place, where I would be coming and spending my recess time. I will not be able to spend that time with you but I will be able to spend the time with your visualizations. In fact, this conversation will play in my head daily, at least once." And she laughed a little, trying to calm herself.

"I shall never ever leave you crying. And who is saying that I am leaving? No one will take our evenings from us. No one will take that bench of the park from us. And about the school hours." I brought her closer to myself. "I will make sure that you have enough memories to talk to and that you never feel alone. And that I can promise."

Her eyes glittered with happiness.

"Do you love me so much?"

"I have stopped measuring indefinite quantities."

We held each other's hands. There was no turbulence in the air. The noise of the going children had drowned. There was complete silence. And in this silence, there were two people who looked deeply into each other, and who were into each other completely. They were not speaking anything, yet they were speaking which only they could understand. I think, every story had its own language which only they could understand.

* * * * *

Just a day before the farewell, a memory day was celebrated in which some of the juniors had to present souvenirs to the leaving batch.

Supriya gave me the souvenir. I owed it to this girl a lot. She had done everything a sister would do to help her brother.

"I am going to miss you bhaiya. I feel so happy that I met someone like you, whom I could call bhaiya. Just in case, if you miss me and meet, my house is going to always remain open for you."

"I know that, I don't need permission to come at my own house."

* * * * *

"Show me that souvenir arav." Aishani was continuously demanding to see it since afternoon.

"its not a very showy thing. It's a sweet and a simple memoir of remembrance."

"I know you very well, *aalsi* arav. You don't want to get up from this bench. Isn't it?"

Oops! Truth was spoken.

"if that's the thing, then come."

I took her to my room and showed her the souvenir. Below the picture of the school, it was written- "vincent academy never forgets its children"

"the message is so lovely."

"yes, it is. Its touching. Don't worry, next year, its your turn. And, oh shit!"

I looked at the clock. It was six. I had made an appointment at the salon for tomorrow.

"I am late for my hair treatment. Bye."

Farewell was a big thing in a student's life. it was one of those rare days when even the one who used to come the most shabbily dressed would come after taking a bath twice. Shopping would start a month ago and the only conversation which could be heard was which colored sari was she purchasing or which company's suit was choosing for the suit.

I never had a facial before but I always wanted to have it. It was one of those childhood dreams in which mummy would say that these things were to be done by grown-ups only. I had asked about this many weeks ago.

A fully groomed man, that's how I would be, and I felt proud visualizing it.

We just messaged- "see you tomorrow"

* * * * *

Supriya was there at the gate. Dressed in cream coloured suit, she looked beautiful. "supriya, is that you under those two kilos of make up?"

"very funny bro, I think, you should pursue standup." She hit me at the back. I pulled her cheeks. "revenge taken." I proudly said.

"where is aishani by the way?"

"hasn't come yet. She must be coming."

I took my number card from the desk. It was fifty six. Alok and aniket had come. Both of them wore tuxedos.

"don't you two feel like staying in the house? The guys who are seen everywhere except in their respective houses."

"that sums it up quite well arav. After farewell, we all have to stay in the house and prepare for the boards so I guess, we have enjoyed our time." Alok proudly announced.

"and don't put blame on us. We have always invited you. But you never came."

They were right. I had other priorities. Aishani, obviously.

"what are you smiling at arav?"

"nothing, just nothing." I went inside the hall. The hall was decorated with green and silver. It looked magnificent. The stage was decorated with flower vase and the theme for the farewell was written above the stage with green. "grow and go green."

Most of the students had come but aishani was nowhere.

"where are you?" I asked impatiently.

"arav, I cant come." This felt as the worst shock of my life.

"what happened aishani? What's the matter?" I had come out of the hall.

"where are you going buddy?" alok asked. I signaled him that I will be back in five.

"I won't come. I am sorry. Bye."

I didn't waste a second and left for her house.

"aunty, what happened? Where is she?"

"upstairs *beta*. I don't know why she is not going. She was so excited to go."

I knocked her door. "mumma, I am not going anywhere. Please don't force me." She was crying.

"aishani?" I softly spoke.

"arav? What?" she opened the door hurriedly.

"why are you here?" she told me to come in. I saw her room. It was all arranged nicely except the green dress which was on the floor. That was the reason, that green dress must have been the cause.

"how can you expect me to enjoy my farewell without you? You had a dance to perform. What about that? Are you mad aishani?"

"yes. I am mad. Now go."

I searched for games in her room. I found scrabble. "do you play this?"

She didn't listen. "hmm, since I am not going anywhere, so I have to spend by playing scrabble all by myself."

"Why aren't you going? Why are you ruining this day?"

"I am enjoying it, sitting with you. I have no problems."

"you are so irritating arav. Why you never listen to me!" she irritatingly said.

Twenty minutes had gone and we were still in the room. we weren't going to the farewell party, that had become clear. She would be scolded badly for not showing up.

She was sitting on the bed, making horrible faces. I was sitting on the study table and watching her expressions.

"*beta* have something." Aishani's mother brought us noodles and soft drinks.

"thank you aunty. We needed it." I nodded.

"here, have it." I passed the bowl to her. She took it. Her face was still gloomy.

"cheer up. I don't like this sad face." I don't know, till when she would smile. It was a tough job to cheer up someone.

"I am sorry." I looked at her. She was mumbling things.

"It's nothing aishani. Nothing at all. Even I would have got bored in the farewell without you. Alok and aniket would have sucked out my patience with their tech-talks. And supriya must have remained busy in anchoring the event. So, just remove that notion that you have ruined my day from your brain."

"why don't you two go out?" aishani's mother had come up to take away the bowls. "yes, that's what I was saying to her. She is not listening."

"aishani, get up and go." Finally, she agreed.

She made up weird, annoying faces but she couldn't do anything. I had her mother's support.

"aunty, we will be back in few hours." "no problem. and aishani, act a little mature."

"act a little mature! That was quite honest. Isn't it aish?"

We were going towards Rajpur road, to the hills. There were some really beautiful scenic places all the way. We had gone to some of them earlier, such as *bhatta fall* and *George everest.* Today, we were going to rajpur, a small village after the mussoorie diversion road.

"you two are so annoying!" aishani kept complaining. She was a child. She would hit anyone and everyone. Innocence had its own perks I guess.

"subway or maggi?" I stopped near the mall. "lets go for a maggi!"

I stopped at the maggi point which was a small shack selling maggi noodles with a cup of tea. And the popularity was massive. Luckily, there were only two other couples there. Privacy guaranteed, I sighed.

"2 maggi and two cups of tea bhaiya." I told the helper boy. He must be ten or eleven, and most probably was the owner's son. Helping in this business was never a choice but the only choice. Three meals a day was still the main objective.

"don't think that much arav." Aishani woke me up from my thoughts. She had noticed my fixed gaze at the boy. She knew that I think a lot.

"thinking will not help, agreed."

"I have something for you." Aishani took out a piece of paper from her denims.

"what is this? love letter? Show me." I was looking at the page. It had many hearts made and something written in a really beautiful handwriting.

"not here. At rajpur."

I gulped down the noodles and the tea as quick as I could. "lets go."

"what's the hurry?" she replied teasingly. That was a relief. She had returned to her original self.

Rajpur had a beautiful park, which was beside a seasonal river. The mild breeze had an intoxicating effect. It was free of city's pace. A perfect place to hear her voice.

We sat on a bench which was facing the river.

"I have waited enough."

"please ignore the grammar." I nodded.

She blushed a little and said softly-"read it on your own. I can't."

I chuckled, "okay. Let's read."

"I hope that you have enjoyed the farewell party and my dance. It has been five months. It looks bit short. So, let me change it. A Hundred and fifty days. Now, that's big. Why does it happen that whenever we get close to someone, the person leaves our lives? Is there a system installed above which tells that, now is the time to separate the two? I feel so. Its just that, the very thought of not seeing you in the school campus with me gives me shivers. I know that You have to move on. You have many bridges to cross and many milestones to create but still, the lover inside me wishes for your physical presence but the admirer wishes you all the success."

I looked at aishani. She was looking at the river. I saw her innocent smile. It will be difficult for me as well to get into the habit of not being able to see this smile.

"I guess, you have made all the preparations for making me cry."

"well, actually yes." She winked.

"The farewell couldn't have been better than this."

* * * * *

There is light after every tunnel, and there is sunlight after every storm. But, after sometime, storm returns. Gone were the happy days. Preboards were to begin in few days. To be honest, I felt that I knew everything. I was prepared for it. But the schedule was a big shock. The sciences had been allotted back to back dates without any break. That was a shocker. Three books of thousand pages per day was a tough job to do. No objection was possible because school was closed.

"It's going to be a tough time. Back to back science exams are hell." I had called aishani, the night before my first exam, which was English.

"I know that you will do well. I have full faith in you."

Next day, I woke up with a call. Aishani was calling me at five in the morning.

"what happened aishani? All well?" I was still very sleepy but was trying my best to sound attentive.

"It's nothing. I had just called up to say all the best to you. Do well and don't get anxious during the paper."

"thank you aishani. I never thought that you would call."

"I will call you every day. Now get up and revise. Bye." And she hung up. That was a nice way to start off the exam days. An honest wish from your loved one.

Everything was going well. She would wake me up every morning and I would revise my chapters and go for the exam. Then came the chemistry paper, which came unexpectedly tough.

Aniket, who sat beside me didn't write a single word. I tried to attempt each and every question. I was thinking that maybe this trick would yield an answer or maybe that trick would yield an answer, but it didn't work that way. I knew that this time, I had done a blunder. I didn't call aishani that day. I felt horrible that day.

Her call came the next day at five. "what happened arav? Was the paper difficult?"

"yes, it was. I think I will be getting very poor marks in chemistry aishani."

"arav, listen. Don't think about that right now. Think about today's paper. Do your best. You can do it."

These words of motivation failed to move me. I thought that I knew everything. I now knew that I didn't know anything.

The preboards ended in the midweek of January. Meanwhile, school had reopened for the other classes. We were called to look at the answer sheets and to collect the admit cards on the thirty first of January. Needless to say, I had failed in chemistry by a great margin.

The whole world started spinning around my head. I knew that this was coming. Hope for the best but be prepared for the worst. It sounded good but it was ideal. The worst had actually happened and I was staring at it frighteningly. This looked like a dead end. It felt pathetic. Even some brats had passed the exam but I hadn't.

"arav, you have to really work hard in these two months. Otherwise, you will not get those marks which we expect from you and which you expect from yourself." Madam sharmila had always been supportive and had always guided me. I nodded.

"madam, I just need aishani for a minute." I was going home but I had to tell her that I had failed.

"how much are you getting in English arav?" madam asked. I was feeling shy in telling it. "not good at all. Below my expectations." "start studying hard. We are expecting a good result from you."

"what happened arav?" aishani had come out.

"I failed in chemistry." That hit aishani hard. Her eyes had widened to the largest extent they could have gone.

"how can you fail? Its impossible for you to fail! I will be damned!"

"I have failed and that's the truth. Nothing can be undone." I was feeling guilty in saying this.

"I will talk to you in night. Bye. Take care."

* * * * *

The whole day had been of no ups but only downs. Mummy had stopped talking. It had come as a big shock, and I felt guilty for that. Even I hadn't expected this downfall. She had immediately ordered to find myself a tutor who would go through my revision for the boards. I had conversed with supriya on the messenger and she had suggested me to join the tuition of madam sharmila. I had agreed to it. After all of this, I called aishani.

"arav, how was the reaction?" her voice sounded low. Was she still sad about my result?

"It was just I had expected. Bad. I have to join madam sharmila's tuitions. I hope things turn good."

"arav, I think we should give free space to each other. I know that this might sound a bit harsh but lets see, lets see if our love can prove itself." She said teasingly, but she was seriously speaking about taking a break. "and to make this more concrete, we shall not be in touch for two months. I am giving my phone to mummy." Was she going mad? Was she in her senses?

"this is the time when I will be needing you the most aishani. I don't know what life will show me in the coming days, but I need your support. A support, which only you can give. But the same person is saying me that I would be gone? Are you not thinking anything about us? Every promise has been undone? Is this a way of testing my love for you? If that's the thing, then it's not good. Not at all good."

"I know that my love loves me this much but you also have to study no? your board exams are just in a month and you need to study and i dont want you to keep thinking about me and degrade your performance. You have to be the best and have to become topper! Imagine aishani! Your boyfriend is a topper, how wonderful would that feel!"

"I will never ever think of you as a distraction for me. How can I even think of that! You were the one who lifted from a phase of sadness and made me enjoy the pleasures of life. You were the one who told me to showcase my talents in the competition. You are my biggest blessing, my infinity."

But but but, who could even think of defeating a girl in a conversation. "enough of your romantic talks Mr arav Sharma. I am not listening to all of this and I am going offline and will not come till the month of march and that is final. Now bye bye and study. Your preboards were not even good, they were infact bad, not even bad but worse, worse for a person like you. Now go and study. And she hung up.

* * * * *

TEN

"Arav, what will you be able to do in just a month? The syllabus of chemistry is literally like pacific. If you don't know where you are heading, then you are bound to loose way and finally get lost." Maam was right, I was too late to react on my failure. Now, the fear of getting a bad percentage was slowly creeping inside my head. A bad percentage would lead to a bad life-that was the conception. A bad mark sheet was the last thing which I wanted.

"is anything possible? Even a short revision would do. Please help me out." I was now shivering and my throat had soared wet. I would have cried that very moment, somehow a ray of hope came along. "you can, if you want, come at six in the morning, it will help you in covering the chapters fast." So, what do we have here, a bitter cold month of January and February, a tuition at six in the morning and to spice it up, we have sarcastic comments everytime I used to glance around my mother. If things had to be this, let it be like this, there was nothing I could do now. All the wrongs I had to undo.

You cannot learn anything unless you have told yourself that you are a big zero. Because after that, you try to put numerals after that zero to make it relevant. Sometimes it becomes a necessity to be hard on yourself. I decided to take the roughest route possible.

Some of my class mates were also studying at maam and they were all surprised to see me. I tried not to bat an eyelid with them. *How can they expect that I cant fail?* I grew conscience about it. Even if I asked a question, the others showed so much shock that afterwards I decided to ask questions after everyone had gone and especially shubhang negi, a wannabe nerd who showed off his "imaginary skills" in solving numericals in chemistry. He was not that bad a guy, but jealousy had crept in.

Aishani never left my thoughts. I used to wonder what she would be doing now and what subjects would she study and most of all, did she missed me everyday? But I tried to keep these thoughts restricted to bed times and those free times when I listened to music and would eventually doze off in the tunes of piano.

Getting up early at six was the hardest thing. If a person could wake up at six without showing any signs of laziness after having slept in a big warm quilt during the month of January, I would have declared him a god. I had set five alarms back to back and I had made up my mind to wake up atleast at the third. I wished I could have said that I made it.

"Are you waking up or not!" I heard my mother shouting downstairs. She had somehow woke up and sounded angry. "This child is a sick person, he doesn't care about his future, he is a brat. Wake up you fool." She kept on saying. I had heard enough. I shouted back at the top of my house – "Can you keep your mouth shout for a while! Can you keep it shut so that I can have any positivity around me!" "very well son, keep on shouting." She said. "just shut your mouth." I got so angry that I banged the door deliberately and didn't close it after going out to the tution.

All of my frustration about the marks, the cold, the tution had burst out. I drove my *activa* slowly in the the thick fog laden roads of dehradun. There were some elderly people jogging, trying to fit themselves In this world which was running in a hurry, milk vans, newspaper distributers, but at large, it was all quite and cold. All the anger had turned into guilt. I should never have spoken rudely with mummy. But, right now, nothing seemed right.

Mummy used to say that the almighty is always taking tests of our calibers and he tests his best students the toughest. This soothed my mind, maybe for a moment. I was not thinking about anything. It was just a blank face going to tuition at six in the morning.

Still drowsy, I somehow grabbed a seat and I slammed my head down, trying to compensate the lost sleep. This sleep was much sweeter. I don't know why, but the sleep before the lectures are not as good as during the lectures. During our physics practicals, one of my classmate, shanky, lulled himself to sleep on the metre scale which was provided. He exclaimed that it was the best sleep he ever had.

I was quickly woken by a cough. Maam had come and she straightaway began with the thermodynamics. "the important ones should be done first and then we will move on to the easier and theoretical."

She told me to do only the important questions and not to divulge in any irrelevant sections in the chapters for there were too many topics which were beyond the scope. I understood what she meant. I had to use my time wisely and not waste it which I had done for the past one year or so. "forget it." She said. "pardon, maam?" she took a good look at my face. "I am a teacher arav and I know about what you are going through and frankly speaking, the best way to handle this is to minimize thinking about your past and think about studies."

Coming back, I kept thinking about the recent events. I felt alone and moreover confused with my life. The road which I had taken was supposed to be easy but due to my errands, it had become a hell of a journey. I couldn't face my mother when I returned that day and went straight into my room. A sudden influx of fright had just crept in. I was sweating. I saw my face in the mirror. "whats wrong with you? tell me! give me a reason! Answer me!" That night, tears were the only available answer.

Since the school was now close for us, we got time to grind ourselves in physics and chemistry. Rest of the subjects are no problem. They never are. And the problem with these subjects were that, we were not taught about our present but what had happened a century ago. Except for the teachers and the parents, this may seem as an excuse, but those who were studying these knew the level of boredom they faced during the class. But, as its said in the Indian system of education- just follow the beats, because those who do not follow the steps are disqualified from the system. Either you leave the country or you become one of those who don't have any name, just an identity- one of the billion Indian. No specific name. just one of a billionth Indian. and the whole ball game is to get an identity. But we middle class people have no fairy tales. We want to be known, but among thousands. Our dreams are middle class and everything else can be said at best- humble. But *padhna toh padega!* And so I had to. That guilt of failing was still there. That was keeping me active. I kept remembering it when I went to the tuitions.

"arav, if you can, you can come at three to cover up the syllabus. You will be able to do it faster." I didn't hesitate. Madam was giving me this opportunity to cover more and more. She had faith on me. She believed that somehow I would pull it off nicely. "definitely, from tomorrow." So, I was going to tuitions three times a day and that too for a single subject. When I came out from the garage where madam taught, I felt a realization. And I hurriedly reached for my *activa* and went to the shiva temple. I went inside and stared at the *lingam*. I had this strange habit of going to this temple and staring at the *lingam*. The flower vendor used to look at me strangely and must have declared me a mental. "I have come to ask for spiritual guidance. What I have to do requires strength and peace. Fill my soul with positivity. *Om namah shivaay*." And I moved out. I kept interrogating while going back my house. Some why's and how's are required to be answered. *The answer lies within* is true.

There were two textbooks for chemistry which I had purchased. One had brilliant numerical problems while the other had an easy and a lucid writing. I opened the numerical one and read the question. I solved it incorrectly. Then I saw the solution. "damnit! I knew the procedure man!" It would not be wrong to say that I was scared of numbers. Numbers would confuse me and ultimately I would loose my confidence and would end up either tearing that page or moving to the next one, which met with the same fate. Now, I had to do. There was no choice of not doing. So I began, by copying the procedure on the blank papers and reciting loudly- "the value of concentration is four centimeter cube and the molar value is twenty. So I have to use the kaulrausch's law." I copied till the last decimal. I saw my page. I tore that page. I took another page and saw the same question. Now I did it myself. I recited the procedure and wrote it and brought the solution till the last decimal. I heaved a sense of relief. "you can do arav, you can." This motivation is never clichéd. Only the individual knows the power of these words. I moved on to the next question, which I did wrong again. I didn't recite the procedure. I tried the next one and got that right. Then I did the second one and corrected myself.

I saw my phone vibrating. Supriya had called. "hows it going bro?" "I am doing excellent. How about you? How is aishani?" "good good. You need to focus more on studies bhaiya. Stop thinking about anyone else and just cram that obese looking chemistry book." "I will do that. Will talk to you later." I noticed something strange in her voice. She was concerned all right. Her emphasis on "anyone" was a bit disturbing. What was she trying to tell? Had aishani said something to her or was I being too concerned?

"alok ass! Return my pen drive!" aniket was yelling at alok at madam's tution. They were the hardcore gamers and movie fanatics. They had drank "the dark knight" and their dessert included "the shawshank redemption" with their appetizers being no less than "shutter island." They had watched it all. I was watching them yell at each other. "aniket ass, listen, when are you returning my hard disk?" "he's got you there aniket." I said, enjoying this casual argument. These were the only source of entertainment which I had. Television and mobile data packs had become ancient. Madam came with some black and white sheets of papers. The other two looked at it with happiness. "review questions!" alok proudly announced. I took one of it. A gateway to marks was open now. It had all types of questions which one could possibly think. It was pure gold. "arav, the more you practice them, the more you will improve." I took all of them. Things were finally falling into place.

After I reached home and read these questions. I was able to answer few of them. I searched through the text book, found out the answers, underlined them and wrote them on the blank sheets. I recalled the answers and they stayed. They didn't fly away like they use to do in the past.

I started writing on the walls of my room. Diagrams and graphs were drawn on the canvas. I was trying to create a masterpiece of my own which I wanted to call it as "self respect." The rough sketch had begun, I felt.

"no one has come." I looked through the gate. The garage lights were out. I didn't go inside. I decided to enjoy this hour. I drove my scooty to the cantonment area and had dimsums with red pepper sauce. I knew it was wrong but that time, it felt right. I needed this get-away and enjoy a small mischief. The word was in a hurry and so was I. maybe I was born a century too late to fit in the society. I laughed at my thought process. It went philosophical when at peace and alone. There were still twenty minutes left. I went ahead, as far as survey of India, leisurely driving at forty, watching the world run wild around me. This was the time when I remembered aishani. When I was enjoying my sadistic pleasures, she would come in my mind and my mind would do the rest. It would recreate the old conversations, create new conversations and I would see her in my front, with all the gossips about the world. "you know that actress who had a breakup with that actor?" I obviously had no idea. I was looking at her, already prepared that she would start her story. "damn you arav! The world is going crazy after their breakup and you are like, you don't give a shit!" I would laugh at that and would bring her closer to myself. "tell me, if I would have known all these things, then what would you have to say?" "oh! Huh! Stop that romance of yours!" "should I stop? Okay then, I will." I would go away from her and sit on the bench. I would wait and count to ten. This was no where close to a fight. It was one of the characteristic of our relation. I would happily sit on the bench, knowing that, she would come and sit beside me within ten seconds. "lets go for a walk." She would say after sitting beside me. "should we? I thought I was not allowed to romance." "Very funny, Mr. Sharma." And that's how we lived during those days. Every walk was memorable. Enough of the nostalgia, I told myself. I drove back home.

Practical exams were a piece of cake. They were easily done. That gave me some confidence that at least, I will not fail. Everyone in the family had given hope, except daddy. "I don't give a thing whether you score a seventy or a sixty but I will definitely be much more happy if you get more than that." Now, sixty was not a goal anymore. It was now about gaining what I had lost- respect. Two weeks were still left for the exam and we were sailing well in the ocean of organics. Extra hours of classes had definitely helped. Chemistry was done here and other subjects were done at home.

"Aishani! Hey!" after so many weeks, I saw aishani while I was going for the evening classes. She looked surprise. "hey arav, how are you doing?" her tone had changed. It was like a dry leaf, all the softness had gone and the chlorophyll had been sucked. Have I made a mistake? I thought so. But I tried to remain unaffected. "oh my god! Such a formal greeting? Your funny bones are gone or what?" she didn't smile or react to the humor. She stood as if I was an unwelcomed guest, trying to fit in. I was disappointed a lot. "got to go, chemistry tuitions." "yes, okay, bye."

My heart sank. It reached the ocean floor of emotions with a thud. All my zeal to study that time ceased. What had happened? What have I done? I had never expected such a behavior from her. Things didn't looked the same as before. How would I know? Had anything happened in her family? I wouldn't know. She had switched her mobile phone off. There was a feeling of negativity. I felt like I had lost her.

I barely concentrated on the chapter that evening. Every time I was doing a problem, her face would appear before me. A flat, unresponsive face. A face which used to smile and blush on even the silliest, non sensical joke, had turned a stone. I spent that night thinking about her. She had broken my momentum. she had sucked all the energy from it.

I called supriya the next day to ask her if anything was wrong with aishani. "no problem. She is very good and cheerful." "okay. Thank you." It didn't feel right to tell her about that incident. I gave up this thought and just waited for time to reveal the truth.

"arav, there is a qawwali performance at the ambedkar program and I have three passes. Want to join?" alok showed the invites three days after the incident. I was not willing to go. I had barely managed to make my mind to ignore aishani for a while but it had cost me my willingness to do anything. I was trying hard to concentrate on the notes. Board exams had come very close. "thank you alok but I will skip. I don't feel like going." "come on arav! Lift your ass a bit and get out. Get a life. Its only a qawwali, not a cocktail dinner for god sake!" who doesn't want to enjoy an evening with friends but I resisted this temptation or had to resist the temptation. I would never get permission from mummy to go. Still I gave a nod in approval.

"I will ask her straightaway. I want to go to see the performance." I rehearsed it while getting back to house. I tried it with different words and tones. Even a small approval was a herculean task for me.

"mummy, alok has arranged for passes for a qawwali program. Can I go?" I asked her at the door itself. She was quiet for a while. "you can go if you want to. But the coming exams are to be given by you. Your future depends on these exams. But, if you still wish to go, then I have no problem." That "no problem" itself was a big problem. When mothers say that they have no problem, it means that they have a big problem and you are not to go for anything, because if you fail to give a good performance in the exams, then this will always be taunted upon. "okay, I will go." I said loudly and went upstairs. I made up my mind to take the risk.

Ambedkar stadium was a five kilometer journey. After many weeks, I had gone to a different route than my usual home to tution route. Alok and aniket were on one scooty and I was on the other. It was evening time and fog was settling over dehradun. It became hazy while returning from the venue. I was pleasantly surprised with the massive audience which had come to listen to the performers. We seated ourselves in the second row. I hoped that the show was worth a gamble.

Soon, musicians came on the stage. Tabla, harmonium, dholak, lyre and sitar players seated themselves on the stage. The singers came dressed in crisp silk kurta pajamas. They bowed their heads and touched the harmonium for blessings. I was fascinated by their devotion. I had never seen a guitarist touching his guitar for blessings. Maybe that's why, many didn't understand Indian music. It has a soul like a human being.

"mai bhi naachu, manau soniya, toh karu na parwah bulleya." The performance had started with so much energy that some people had their heads spinning with the beats. They had completely surrendered themselves to the music. With each song, the positivity with each couple was increasing. I closed my eyes and listened. It was fantastical. I had no knowledge about singing but this kind of music didn't require any special tricks to understand. The lyrics had only one message to convey, which was to submit yourself to the supreme power. I fell deep into it and listened the remaining songs with my eyes closed. It was pleasing. It was telling me to look at the bigger picture.

Hardly a week was left for the exams to begin. Alok and aniket would sometimes show up in tuitions. They had arranged for computer as well as English tutors. Everyone was in a hurry to get in the batch of a retired English professor or to get in a batch of a computer teacher of their schools. I didn't feel the need to get in these tutorials where kids were in the batch of forties and fifties. I kept reading literature during my free time. That was proving to be an effective method.

School exams had started in Vincent academy. I wanted to say an all the best to aishani but I was unable to contact her. My bad luck again. "supriya, all the very best for the exams. Tell aishani that I have send my regards." "thank you bhaiya, and yes, I will." That was the best I could do.

Three days before the first exam, all of the students came to the tuition and asked for various tips and tricks. "do what you know and try what you don't. and don't cheat. Control your devil within." That evening was spent in these what to do and how to do queries. Everyone was excited and nervous about boards. "finally! The time has come which will be undoubtedly sickening and will screw our brains." "alok, just shut up. Your wit is not witty. Thinking about wit, I have to start that annoying Shakespeare play. Who the hell gives a play in a curriculum!" "guys, accept it. We have to read it. Whether we do it willingly or not. But the fact is- Shakespeare is going to decide our percentage." There was a pause after this. I was thinking about aishani and the promise. As soon as the exams would get over, aishani and I would meet as planned. I was waiting for that day like anything. This distance had proved my dependence on her. Without her, it felt awful. I hoped that she felt the same. Emotions don't change suddenly. Or did they?

With three days left for the English paper, I finally opened the workbook of the stories, poems and the plays. The critical appreciation given in them was hailed important by the teachers. During this time, every word said by the teacher is hailed important. Needless to say, I was "shakespearezoned."

The first exam has to go good, otherwise the rest of the exams won't go. And to crack the first exam, everyone had arrived an hour before the exam and were discussing the previous year questions. "last time, they had asked the theme of the play, wondering what they might ask this time?" "have you done that Last scene where Romeo and Juliet die?" I wanted to say to them to get lost from my eyes but I had to keep a half baked smile and say- "oh! That one! I just forgot that part. Rest of it is complete." His shocking eyes were more shocking to me than his shock. This all made me nervous. That's why I wanted to stay away from them.

After English, the exams would come and go. The nervousness had finished. The chemistry paper came as a pleasant surprise. Hard work seemed to have paid off. Now, I was in a hurry to finish the papers and meet aishani. Her exams were to finish the next day of my last exam.

"So, Ms. Aishani, did you miss me? No, no, no, it was too blunt. Something else. Hey aishani! How are you? Damn! Why am I sounding so formal?" even the man in the mirror seemed unimpressed by my greeting. "can you be a little more casual?" "I am trying, arav." My inner and the outer self got into an argument. "Okay. Leave it. Let's do it once more. Hello aishani! How did the exams go? Mine went good. This sounds a bit better. Isn't it?" the man in the mirror was pleased. I hoped that she would start the conversation.

"hey supriya! How is my sister doing?"

"oh my god! Buttering! What's the catch?"

"no catch stupid. Leave that. How is aishani doing?"

There was a second's pause. "She is good. Okay, you know, anuj of my class, approached me and asked me if we could hangout! Isn't it great?"

"yes, it is. That's some news." I had noticed her tone which had suddenly changed. She had changed the topic about aishani again and that made my heart sink further. I was thinking the same thing which every other person would have thought. Had she ended the relationship from her side? I didn't want to believe but I felt that this was coming.

Supriya kept talking about her studies and every possible gossip she had heard about girls and guys but I barely heard a word. I hung up.

"Mummy, I am going to the park. Will come back soon."

"what's the matter?" "Nothing, nothing." I would tell her everything after some time. I sat on the bench and thought about it. Supriya knew everything. Aishani must have said something to her. I had to meet and clarify this fix.

It's amusing to see that when you think negative, your entire surrounding dyes itself into grey and dull textures. Everything in the park which looked greener, looked dead. Dry leaves scattered everywhere. My senses were aware that there were a lot of green leaves around but would they see it? No. they wouldn't.

Amidst all this turbulence, I gave my last exam. All of us shouted in joy. Even the invigilators were happy. A rarity. These days had been difficult. Relatives calling, house arrests and a relationship at a critical conjecture. Relatives wouldn't call till the results, so it was not a problem anymore. House arrest was over. Only thing which needed sorting was with aishani.

I turned back at the school gate and looked at the entire campus. It had been a long journey in here. Something made me to touch the gates. It was nostalgia. You cry when you come to this place and you cry when you leave this place. "Sometime later, I will come back." I promised these painted walls.

alok was waiting for me at the parking. He was going to pune for his higher studies. "here you go buddy." we did the cool handshake which guy best friends did. "I am going to remember your pen drives." "die in hell. How about you? Any plans?" "I have applied for the science college at bihar. Let's see what happens." We, boys suck at showing emotions. Even if your best friend was leaving you, the most you could do was to give a pat on the back and say good luck.

I saw him going. I went in the opposite direction.

"Finally, Boards are over. Go to hell class twelve." Supriya laughed at this emotional throwup. "I understand bhai. This was one hell of a journey for you. My condolences." She teased. "shut up. Listen now. let's meet tomorrow at the café near the school. Bring aishani along." She was silent for a while. "I will come but I don't know about aishani." "Alright. It's decided then. At twelve."

Supriya was not coming to meet me. She was coming to tell me that aishani had ended the relationship. It was just going to be a formality about getting told. I had known this for a while now. I just had to endure it. Why? This why was still not answered.

I kept looking at the ceiling all night long. I barely slept.

Night time is a funny time. It ends quickly for those who are in love. While, it is punishing for the others. I had experienced the former. I was experiencing the latter.

"bhaiya, how much time left for the bell to ring?" I was standing at the school gate. I had decided to confront aishani then and there. She had to explain. No one walks away like this. "five minutes." The little kids started to come out. Soon, the gate was crowded with parents and the cab drivers. I sat on my scooty which I had parked near the gate. I was looking at each coming student. Supriya was the first one to show up. "supriya, where is she? I want to talk to her." She hurriedly said, "Come with me." She took me to the café. "bhai, you need to understand that..." "That it's over. Isn't it?" I smiled while completing her unfinished sentence. "I knew that this was coming. I really had this suspicion when you didn't talk about aishani and told me to concentrate on studies. I should have been..." I couldn't say more. Emotions which had bundled up came out from the eyes. But we can't cry in public. People considered it as a sign of weakness. "What now? Should I hit myself against the wall and act like a person mad in love? No, I will message her right now, in front of you."

I checked my messenger to see if she was online. She was. She had just changed her display picture. I send her a "hi." She read it but didn't reply. I began typing furiously, putting all my anger in the message, asking all the why's and what's from her. But the message was not received. The display picture was gone. A grey figure replaced the smile. I called her. It kept saying that the number was busy. It kept saying to call again later. I tried again. Once more.

"Don't try bhai. She won't."

"GO TO HELL YOU TWO!"

I stormed out of the café.

* * * * *

"I am sorry supriya. It just came out. I was not under control of my anger."

"It's understandable. Anyone would have behaved the same way. Are you okay now?" "I am not okay. How can I be okay?" it made me laugh out loudly. Supriya must have declared me a mad man.

"control yourself Bhaiya. It's not the end of the world. You will get a better person in your life." "I am not buying clothes that if this didn't last long, then the next from a branded shop would last longer! When you say forever, it should mean forever. Otherwise, why to break hearts by fake promises."

"Agreed bhaiya. But staying gloomy forever is not a solution as well."

She tried well to console me but it didn't work out. No one but the sufferer knows the suffering.

"mummy, I want to tell you something."

"what happened?"

"mummy, there is a friend of mine."

"friend? Is it a girl?"

"oh please mummy, not that thing. Anyways, it's not about a girl." A necessary lie.

"you should stop thinking so much about these friends. They are not trustworthy. They are temporary. They will leave you one fine day and you will then find someone else. This cycle goes on and on."

I had framed a different perspective that friends were for life and if a friend went away from your life, then, he was never a friend. He was just an acquaintance. Was my ideology a cliché? Was I living in my own world which I considered perfect?

Infinity for me was not endless. It was a close loop, which started and ended at the same point.

Aishani had become my infinity and I had accepted that. Now I was being told that, infinity was just a made up word. It had no connection with the reality.

* * * * *

"Just ask her once, please." A week had gone by and the only conversation I had with supriya was to find out the reason.

"No, no and no. I won't"

"You know what, she had told you. You know the reason. And you have been told to say mum about it. I just want to know why you have been told to stay quiet."

"Why do you think that I know?"

"Don't play games with me like this please. I request you to please tell me."

They had no right to keep secrets from me.

"I will send a screenshot in your messenger account. You will know."

That was better. At least I would be able to know what she was thinking that time and maybe I would be able to resolve that issue and maybe, maybe she would come back. That, though was a long shot, but was worthy for a try.

The messenger popped open. The screenshot read-

"Never had I thought that I would date you Mr. Sharma. You looked so boring and tired of your own life that I felt scared to talk to you. I mean, how a person could live like this! Without any friends and just eating his lunchbox near the stage! Gradually, I realized that you had a very vivid imagination of your future. You wanted to do something good to yourself. You wanted to excel. You wanted to earn for yourself. And when I came into your life, you made me your infinity. I was on cloud nine."

Another screenshot came-

But I felt that I was a burden for you. It felt like I had become your weakness. I knew that you were a person of words, but I didn't know that when you had said that I was your infinity, you would mean it this seriously that you would change yourself so much to provide me with all the happiness. Arav, you have to study more. You have to cross many bridges. You have to lead so many battles. You cannot limit yourself on me. You cannot make me your infinity. That's why I am going away from your life. I hope that you will do all the things which you have planned.

Tears were flowing hysterically. How unlucky I was. I couldn't even cry properly because mummy would hear it. I closed my eyes and let the tears drip on my cheeks. They kept coming and I kept wiping.

"supriya, please forward this message to aishani."

"okay. I will."

"You were never a burden for me. You were never a problem for me. When I said that I will be with you, I had never put conditions. Never had I said that I was unable to do well because of you. A person sacrifices his desires for love. That's the only thing which separates us from wild animals. Try and understand."

"She is not listening bhaiya. She says that she has thought about it a lot and that her decision is final. She has told me to tell you to forget her."

"Forget her? That's an excellent plan! Forget her. What were the things I needed to forget about her? Forget her face?

Forget her voice? Forget those moments which we had spent? Forget those assignments which we did together? Forget that we went to the park every evening? EVERY EVENING!"

"I can't do anything bhaiya."

"I know you can't. You tried a lot. Thank you."

"Shut up bro!"

* * * * *

The first problem after the break up was that I had nothing to do to deviate my mind to other things. How much time a person could spend on dusting? How many movies could he watch? Or how many songs would he listen all day?

I would eat up supriya's mind whenever she came online. But for how long would she be there to listen? One day, she too would leave like everybody else.

There were these friends with whom I tried to start a conversation. But the conversations turned stale after three to four sentences. It would start with a generic "hello" and would abruptly come to an end with "hmm" or a "k."

No one had approached me to interact with interest as much as aishani used to. She would keep on explaining the things she had done that day that I was bound to react and the conversation would never stop. It had been two weeks but my favorite past time was to look at the caller id of my phone. I had put her photograph as the caller id so that her display picture would show her photograph and not just a grayish figure.

She had promised me to stay forever and that was exactly what she had taken away from me.

I came out of the house after many days for a change. All the streets were storehouses of memories. Every road was walked upon. Every road had heard the giggles of a guy and a girl who would walk till the end in the evenings. The echo of laugh still loud and clear in my ears.

Park looked the same. There were children playing and some aunties who used to gossip about us whenever they would see us. Their face would turn pale and their eyes would swell with surprise as if saying- how dare that you sit in this park together. We would reply them with a wide smile.

I would see the sunset daily in the park and would quietly return. I never saw her in the park. Maybe she knew that I would come in the park, maybe she knew that I was waiting for her. Maybe. Everything was a maybe.

* * * * *

"why didn't you tell us, you asshole" aniket yelled upon me. "I mean, you are such a disgrace to be called a friend. You should have simply said. We would have done everything we could to make you feel positive. But you kept it hidden for eight months!"

I had never told them about aishani. After the cancelled book session, no one paid heed to it and ultimately it ended. And with it, all those conversations which we used to have during the book reading sessions.

Now it was alok's turn. "don't say anything to him. He hardly cares. He thinks that he can bear all the pain and still live happily. If you don't want to tell us anything, don't tell, but let me tell you one thing. You are not a superhuman who can't feel any emotion. You are just an ordinary person."

I couldn't say anything. I knew that I had made a mistake by not telling them. I had broken their trust. I felt ashamed of myself.

"Now, get up. We are going to robber's cave and you are coming with us."

"do I have a choice?" "of course you have. Yes and yes. Get up now."

a bike ride with friends Is the most enjoyable thing when you need to ease out on your life. and to increase the fun, aniket had installed speakers in his royal enfield and played Punjabi songs. That was a welcome change from a guy who always listened to the beatles.

I had met them after a long time. I had virtually disconnected myself from the entire friend circle. I never felt like talking with classmates on messenger or hangout with them for real. All I wanted was oblivion. The thing which I hated was the thing which I now wanted.

"you know guys, we never came here." It just came out involuntarily. I had associated every place with her. This was one of the places where we haven't come. And will not come ever.

"someone just throw him into water please." Alok said. "have you come with us or with her memories which gives you nothing except pain?"

"I am sorry guys. That came out unintentionally." They looked at me with sympathy in their eyes. They had believed that I would never get into this but I had fell into it and had fell badly.

We walked in the shallow waters of robber's cave and reached the waterfall. Aniket pushed me and I fell in the ice cold water fall. It stung like a hundred bees. "you will pay for this." I yelled. And pushed both of them in water. They laughed hysterically at this.

Seeing them laugh, I realized that they were doing it for me. It was all an attempt to make me happy. I started laughing with them. I laughed at myself. I was thinking about a person who had left me over those people who would never let me leave.

Boy's bike tour are incomplete without dimsums. We had five plates of steamed dimsums. They were divine as usual.

"stop thinking and start living bro. we don't want to see you gloomy all the time." Alok said while dropping me at my house.

"I will. Thank you buddy."

My efforts to forget the past started with connecting with old friends. Since they had no idea what was going in my life, I could speak freely and even make jokes about myself.

"are you still single?" one of the classmates with whom I was conversing after four months asked.

"yes Man! I am so very single."

That helped a bit, though not much. Still, the biggest stress relief was talking with supriya. I had especially asked her to talk as random as she could.

She was a professional at this as she gossiped about everyone a lot.

I stopped listening to bollywood's top twenty heartbreak songs or things like that. I now listened more English.

"have you met her since?" that answer fucked the whole thing up.

I yelled at supriya. "you dumb girl. Why you asked about her? Are you trying to tease me or instigate me to talk to her? No, I will never talk to her. In fact, I have deleted her contact."

Yes, I had deleted her contact. She was no more in the list. But that single question was enough to remember about her. I felt a huge anguish. Maybe she had unblocked me? I asked aishani's contact from one of her close friends, vaishali.

My heart skipped a beat when I saved her contact. In anticipation that she may have unblocked me, I saw the same grey figure which I had seen some weeks ago for the first time.

My heart felt heavy at that point. I cried after so many days.

False hopes are more futile than despair full of conviction.

* * * * *

Every night, she comes in my dream and talks. Every night, she would ask me how I was? I gave the same answer every time- I am incomplete without you. A sleeping eight if cut from the middle was a zero. That's exactly how I am without you.

And she would disappear.

I saw myself running across the beach, in desperation. Desperation of finding someone.

> *He lost the pace and got lost in the race*
> *His life would have been great if only*
> *Things would have happened as he wanted.*

There is no one at the beach. He is all alone. Yet he is trying to find someone.

These visualizations often get mixed. Sometimes, he sees himself going down with the sea current and ending his life.

He sees himself lost in the city. Bizarre lights and criss crossing roads make his head spin. Its night time and everyone has slept. But he sees himself walking at night, in the loneliest of roads.

He hears the wail of the siren, coming from a distant area. He wastes his time on looking at the flicker of the street light.

What pleasure he takes in at observing it, only he knows.

He had opened her contact id once again and once again, like many other nights, he went a year back, and inflicted the pain of remembering her.

At least, give me a reason to let you go

Never did she replied. A silence loomed.

ELEVEN

I didn't know when I fell asleep, looking at the mobile screen. This had become a sort of a routine. Just remembering her, knowing that she won't come, but still, but still, some things feel so good, their mere false presence make us happy. This was my false hope. To see her again, to see her talking to me again. One year ago, things looked different. Just three hundred and sixty five days had changed everything.

Next morning, I drove my scooty to supriya's house. I didn't even care to call her and tell about my arrival. "sorry uncle, if it wasn't urgent, I would have never come without calling." "its ok *beta.*" I hurried upstairs to supriya's room. She was still sleeping. "I am having sleepless nights and look at her, just look at her." I shrugged her shoulders hurriedly. "Are you waking up or should I call the police?" "fuck bro. you just ruined my dream. What's the hurry. My god! You have straightaway come to my room? Are you like mad?" she was looking puzzled. "listen up, I don't care if I entered the room without permission or not. I need your help and I need it right now." "is it about aishani?" there goes my sister. "I need a confrontation. I want to meet her. I need to talk to her. Do you understand?" "relax bro, just calm down first, let me dress up, then we will sort this out nicely. Get in the kitchen, eat whatever you want. Give me ten minutes." I went to the kitchen, aunty was preparing the breakfast. "it will be ready in five minutes arav, by the way, what has happened?" how can I tell you aunty! I made up a story about school notes which some friend of mine required urgently. She was not convinced but she gave a slight nod. You cant fool a parent after all.

"I need to confront aishani, just for the first and last time. I just want to talk to her in person and then I will be at peace. We have not even talked since then. Its bit of an odd thing *na*?" "yes, it is." She smiled weakly. Supriya knew my pain. She was a sister. Sisters just know it. "what have you planned? What will you do?" "I will not do anything. You will call her right now and you will tell her to meet outside the school gate today." "are you mad bro! she wont come. She will get suspicious." "come on! Try it once and even if she gets suspicious, I don't give a damn." I was very adamant.

"okay. I am calling her." "put the loudspeaker on."

She called and the speaker came to life with the similar sound. She picked it up. It was overwhelming to hear her voice. I felt like crying. Not because for what she had done, but because, I missed her so much. "hey aishani, I am calling you up so that we can meet today at the school gate?" "is everything okay supriya?" aishani asked with concern. Weird, I thought. She is concerned about others. But, not me. Not us. I gave a huge sigh. Supriya warned me to stay quiet. "yes aishani, everything is rock and roll. Just wanted to hangout." "sounds good. I will be there at ten. Bye."

I was in a big state of confusion. I had taken a very big step. If we had been talking regularly, this meeting would have meant nothing. But, after so many months, it was something else. Something more nerve breaking. And I knew, aishani would get a bigger shock when she would see me suddenly. But, it had to happen, sooner or later. The confrontation is necessary.

I reached the school gates at ten. The place where thousands of memories present, stood behind. Those classrooms which I had shown her were all there. A chill went up through my spines. I hadn't moved on still. No sign of girls as I kept rewinding my memories. Supriya finally came. She parked her scooty. I waved off, there was no need to say sorry for coming late. The big thing was that she was there. "she must be coming." I said. "this is going to be bad." Supriya said, looking at me. "I know that. But I cant accept silence without sentence." I politely replied. "she is coming. I see her." In her bright green top and black denims, I saw her after months. She hadn't changed.

She stopped about thirty yards before. She was taken aback. Her face had turned pale. All her face had reddened. I knew that had to happen. You feel damned after seeing ex-boyfriends suddenly, isn't it? She approached slowly. "hey supriya! How are you?" the awkwardness was evident in her voice. "I am good. Listen, arav bhaiya wanted to meet you, so I just called and arranged for this meeting." Thankyou supriya for that, I saw her. She made it easier for me. "why you wanted to meet me?" she asked bluntly. I was angry. "you are asking me that question? how dare you ask that? If there is nothing left, then, you must have said. No one leaves like that." But I didn't say these.

I stood in front of her and said- I don't know why you did this to our relationship. It was not your fault. It wasn't mine either. So, there is no point of apologizing to each other. We shared a very sweet relationship. We never fought. We never said loudly to each other. I think, we were too perfect for each other that we were not fit to live with each other. I have read some quotations which said- those relationships are the best in which one person is mature and the other one is little immature. Maybe that was missing in ours. We were both seriously stupid." I chuckled. "she smiled a bit. My voice had started to crack. Still I went on- I will not say that I want to have you again. Somedays before, I wanted to do that. Not now. I have understood that some things are meant to happen, and some people are meant to come in your life. They come, make you feel special and then they move ahead. You did your part great. It was me who thought that you were meant to stay forever." She burst out crying. "I had no intention of making you cry. Instead, I want to say thank you very much for coming in my life. I had not come to say anything to you about those screenshots which you had sent. I have no right to ask you that. You wrote what you felt and I said what I felt. I think I'm done."

I cleared my throat and wiped my tears. Supriya was holding her hand. Aishani was crying hysterically.

"aishani, you are a good person, remember that."

"please bhaiya, you should go. Just go." "yes, I was going anyway." And I broke into a run. Last thing I saw was supriya hugging aishani, consoling her.

I ran as fast as I could. I could just see the road with no thoughts except running. There was complete blankness. A perfect void. After entering vasant vihar, did I finally stopped. I was panting heavily. I reached for the handpump, splashed the cold water which did brought me back in senses. I sat on a bench. I felt like calling supriya and ask about aishani, felt like apologizing. I was too rude. I was blunt in my emotions. "no arav, you didn't make any mistake. You said what you wanted to say. Now, there is nothing left. Actual breakup has happened now." the person within me counseled. I took out my mobile, scratched the sim card and threw it away in a dustbin.

I hugged my mother and father. They were puzzled to see this gesture. They were the only one who was there and who will be there for me, no aishani or supriya were to remain forever. And if they were to remain forever, then they would not have bragged about being together forever, instead, they would have stayed. Parents never say that we will remain forever with you. Yet, they are the only ones who stay.

"Daddy, I want to go to Patna and study there."

"What made you say so?" aishani, I thought. That's why I was going out of this place. To forget, to stop thinking about her every single time when I was alone, and move ahead.

"I want a change of air and change of people's faces as well. And you have to get a new sim card for me, so, buy me a card there." I laughed. I had never told him about aishani but I felt that he knew it. His facial expression would turn into a cynical one with a raise eyebrow whenever he would hear that I was going out with a friend. Yet, he never said anything.

Banaras was my native place. Fourteen years ago, we had come to this city. This city accepted us. We came with little luggage, lived in a *dharamshala* nearby the railway station for two months. We purchased a two wheeler only after eight months. But steadily, we progressed as the city did. I was going away from this city.

I spent my last days in dehradun with alok and aniket. We went to the falls, discussed our future. Alok also made us pledge the friendship code that we will always remain in contact with each other. I thought that I could give upon them. They were still there. Besides that, how could I have forgotten dimsums! And Buddha temple. I tried to go to as many places where I had memories. I went to my temple then. I had been going to this temple since class six. It was my custom, before the commencement of the session and before exams, I had to go. When you want something desperately, you start believing in everything which promises you that it would help in getting it. "Nothing to say today. Be with me like you always are."

My application for admission was accepted by Science College, Patna. I had to report as soon as possible. I would be living in a hostel there. Mummy was little nervous about hostel food and ragging but I had to go, so even she couldn't do anything about it. She will understand gradually. There comes a time when a child has to go outside his house. That time had finally come.

"Ready?" mummy asked. I gave a positive nod. The train slowly made its way into the terminal. I had two airbags and a backpack. Backpacks had the usual contents- a laptop to give everyone a perception that you are a tech-savvy guy, a mini music player to give you the tag of a cool person, and a pair of headphones, including chargers for everything. Sides of the airbag included loafers and the small pouches were used to keep the toiletries. This is the standard packing code for Indians.

"I have kept biscuits and wafers. Don't eat anything offered by a stranger. And call immediately when you reach." "Obviously mummy, I will." I reassured her that everything will be good. "Be cautious about those spoilt brats in the college. Believe in your conscious." "Yes daddy. I think you both should go. The train's about to leave." We came out from the coach. The station was lit with halogen lights and the digital signboards. The platform was almost deserted. Everyone had seated themselves. The passenger in the train and the visitor's in their vehicles. The engine gave a loud and piercing honk. "You should get in now." I nodded. Touched their feet and went inside. A sudden jerk and we started moving. I kept waving them till the train left the station. There were some people on the other side of the coach. My compartment was empty. I looked outside but it was just darkness. There was no need to look for it outside. Darkness was readily available within.

I believed that everything happened for our own good. The past experiences had altered this statement a bit. Everything happened for our own good till everything which happens to us is good. When things turn ugly, then you stop believing these moral boosting thoughts. Only two things can then happen to you. Either you break down or you try to join those broken pieces. As the train chugged out of the station, I turned off the compartment's light and dozed off to sleep. Life had to go on.

Printed in the United States
By Bookmasters